THE LAST

OF THE

WHITE ANTS

Pattie Pink

Order this book online at www.trafford.com/05-0413
or email orders@trafford.com

Most Trafford titles are also available at major online book retailers.

Front and Back Cover Photographs
GULE WAMKULU DANCERS
Two very rare photographs of complex dances linked closely to traditional initiation ceremonies.

Note for Librarians: A cataloguing record for this book is available from Library and Archives Canada at www.collectionscanada.ca/amicus/index-e.html

ISBN: 978-1-4251-9166-5

We at Trafford believe that it is the responsibility of us all, as both individuals and corporations, to make choices that are environmentally and socially sound. You, in turn, are supporting this responsible conduct each time you purchase a Trafford book, or make use of our publishing services. To find out how you are helping, please visit www.trafford.com/responsiblepublishing.html

Our mission is to efficiently provide the world's finest, most comprehensive book publishing service, enabling every author to experience success. To find out how to publish your book, your way, and have it available worldwide, visit us online at www.trafford.com/10510

www.trafford.com

North America & international
toll-free: 1 888 232 4444 (USA & Canada)
phone: 250 383 6864 • fax: 250 383 6804 • email: info@trafford.com

The United Kingdom & Europe
phone: +44 (0)1865 487 395 • local rate: 0845 230 9601
facsimile: +44 (0)1865 481 507 • email: info.uk@trafford.com

10 9 8 7 6 5 4 3 2 1

FOREWORD
Professor Colin Baker (HlaSS)

If one gathered together many of the expatriates who had lived in Malawi and asked them in which decade in the past century they would most liked to have lived, or would now like to re-live, there would, naturally, be a great range of responses, and a great number of reasons and motivations for their choices.

Some would prefer the earliest days when there were no cars, no trains, no aeroplanes; when tsetse-resisting shank's pony, gently swinging and suddenly-bumping machilas, and oft-grounded paddle steamers, were the irregular means of travel; when wild game was there in plenty to view or to shoot for the pot or to provide trophies to hang on the lime-washed mud walls of their houses; when lighting was by Hurricane or Tilley lamps; when drinking waters was boiled and filtered through chalk candles in a ceramic filter and kept cool in a canvas bag; when perishable food was kept in a charcoal-lined box; when one's domestic staff numbered at least half a dozen; and when all bread was home made – with coarse flour and dried hops.

Others would prefer more recent days, when at least in towns, there was a wide range of goods available in modern shops; when there were cinema shows to enjoy; when kitchens were equipped with all manner of up-to-date electrical gadgetry; when cars could be driven comfortably for long distances on tarmac roads; when one's children flew out from England in jumbo jets for the school holidays; and when next-door-neighbours really did live next-door rather than fifty miles away through the bush.

The range of preferences would be legion, yet it is very likely that many, when asked in which decade they would prefer to have lived, or would now like to re-live, would chose neither the very early nor the very recent days. Instead, many would select the 1960s, for very different reasons from those attributed to the sixties in Britain.

What was there special about the 1960s in Malawi? Primarily, it straddled two major eras: the end of the colonial and the beginning of the independent, both exciting, though in very different ways.

Young men and women from other countries, mainly Britain, were still being recruited into the civil service; they still had development tasks to perform but now they did so increasingly with Malawian colleagues and with the object of training their successors. At the beginning of the decade, the autonomy of Nyasaland was shared with the Federal Government and the demise of that regime at the very end of 1963, though regretted by some, was but briefly lamented by many and not lamented at all by others. They were interesting days, but many would feel not nearly as interesting, and exciting, as those that followed, with the swift move to independence, the l964 cabinet crisis, the creation of the Republic and the incursion of overseas aid agency staff and expert advisers, numerous both in the number of individuals and in the number of countries from which they came. Malawi had never experienced such a wide range of nationalities.

I have a strong feeling – though I have not asked her – that among those who, given the opportunity to re-live a decade of their choice in Malawi, would select the 1960s - would be Pattie Pink. In her 'White Ants', a fictionalised account of expatriate life there during that decade, she introduces us to, and helps us to get to know, a large number and considerable variety of individuals and many 'characters', but what of the author herself?

Patricia Shelagh Pink, born in Windsor, Ontario, Canada, was educated at a variety of British private schools during the Second World War. Her hopes to proceed to University were thwarted by the priority given to returning soldiers, and instead she studied at a secretarial college and then the Central School of Arts and Crafts in London, where she studied typography and layout. She then worked for A & C Black, publishers in Soho Square, for five years and eventually ran their education department's advertising and promotions. She married Ken Bean in 1952 and had two sons, and together they travelled to Rhodesia in 1958. Three years later, her husband's work took him to Nyasaland, and the family moved with him. Pattie was appointed Publications Officer to the Ministry of Information and was seconded to the Extension Aids Branch of the Department of Agriculture, where she became responsible for the technical production of the monthly magazine, Farm News, together with leaflets, posters, technical books and grass roots training material. She also designed a mobile puppet theatre and carried out visual perception research in collaboration with Kenya and the Audio-Visual Aids Centre in London. She was also responsible for the design of the Ministry of Natural Resources show-winning stands at the 1963 Lilongwe Agricultural Show and the 1964 International Independence Trade Fair in Blantyre.

After leaving Malawi in 1969, now with four children, she returned to Salisbury, Rhodesia and worked as a Production Manager, Account Executive and Associate Director in three major Advertising Agencies. In 1982 she opened her own Public Relations service and for the next twenty years she specialised in scripting, producing and presenting film series for the Zimbabwe Broadcasting Corporation and corporate films for industry and commerce. She also produced and presented a number of radio series and programmes. Over these years she was awarded Television Presenter of the Year 1991; Communicator of the Year 1993 (A Fellow of Zimbabwe Institute of Public Relations), Radio Presenter of the Year 1994 (Information and News). She served on the founding committee of The Positive Health Association and held the post of voluntary Chairman for 25 years and was presented with the Rotary Paul Harris award for her 15 years voluntary work with a disadvantaged African community.

Pattie married Norman Pink in 1983 and they now live in Verwood in East Dorset. Between them, they share six children and twelve grandchildren, spread over Australia, South Africa, Zimbabwe, Ireland, France and England.

These biographical details add a background to the fascinating story that Pattie Pink now tells in "The Last of The White Ants

THE LAST OF THE WHITE ANTS (Zizwa Zoyera)

This book has been written in loving tribute to all those extraordinary British Colonial Civil Servants who, over the last century, have carried, with great confidence, the banner of 'The British Way of Life' to Africa.

I have often questioned their right to do this, but, given the sacred British Colonial Civil Service Commandment, 'We must be right, we're British!' I could never fault their courage and unwavering triplicated application of the British Civil Service Rules to several decades of bemused, unfailingly courteous people of Africa, at the turn of the nineteenth Century.

Yes they were courteous and extremely obliging you know, and, in case you want to argue, listen to this. In the late 1880s down the road from Maravi, in a country eventually called Rhodesia, an obliging local tribesman, responded to the question 'Found any yellow stones around here', by leading two white prospectors to what would eventually become one of the richest gold mines in the country, the Globe and Phoenix. The prospectors, much to the astonishment and dismay of the guide, immediately fenced off the area as their property...and what was the local reward? Two blankets and a job for 2/6d a month, for heaven's sake!

To those readers who think they can recognise some of the characters in the book, you may be right, you may be wrong, but just remember that I wrote this book out of great affection and undying admiration for each and every White Ant of Nyasaland. They all deserve to be remembered for their very unique and endearing qualities and sometimes frankly odd characteristics and strange habits. I remember them all with clarity and love. Forgive the poetic play on some events and situations but I hope that the gentle manipulation of facts makes for a more interesting read.

ACKNOWLEDGEMENTS

Many people have been involved in the birth of this book and deserve heartfelt thanks: in particular, John Bishop and Ed Usher who installed (and taught me how to use) a computer donated by RUKBA, the Royal United Kingdom Beneficent Association; a magnificent organisation, recently renamed Independent*Age*, which assists retired professionals through the leaner golden years.

This book would never have been completed without the tolerance and hands-on work of my husband and family. Very special thanks also go to Nic Spiers of Spiers Electronics, Verwood for his creative desktop design and layout, and for never losing his cool! Thanks too James Bowen of Cork University and Erica and Tony Standen, old friends from Zomba days, who gently advised, corrected detail and spelling and gave much needed encouragement on a regular basis.

But it was Professor Colin Baker of Glamorgan University, internationally acknowledged as the major historian on the events and personalities leading up to the Independence of Malawi, who played the most significant role in the final production of this book. Certainly without his constant encouragement and generous sharing of facts and figures, this book would never have been finished.

THE LAST OF THE WHITE ANTS

In 1955 the AFRICAN NATIONAL CONGRESS, under the radical leadership of Henry Chipembere and Kanyama Chiume, invited Doctor Hastings Banda to return to Nyasaland and lead the country to Independence. In fact he did not return until 1958.

CHAPTER ONE
SINCLAIR GETS HIS MARCHING ORDERS

Sinclair Brown was bored. The slightly opened curtains revealed that it was a typical day in Dulwich, raining and almost certainly cold and he had no plans whatsoever. Yes, he was bored out of his mind. He pondered upon his hopes for a career in the colonial service, his somewhat meagre qualifications and the endless interviews and realised, with regret, that Her Majesty must have given the thumbs down. No positive decision could have taken this long. Certainly the hoped-for OHMS letter had never arrived. Pity that, when he felt he had quite a suitable background, minor public school, agricultural diploma and not bad at amateur theatricals too. Lance, his school pal already working in Nyasaland, said that a spot of experience on the boards was a real ace card in Zomba, the tiny capital. Sinclair sighed deeply. 'Shame really.'

His mother, downstairs in the kitchen preparing breakfast, went to the foot of the stairs and called up to him. "Come on Sinclair, it's 10 o'clock and I've got to go to the shops." Sinclair pushed back the bedclothes and then he heard it. The postman's knock! Would it be today! He heard his mother go to the front door and there was a moment of silence, and then, "Sinclair come down quickly, there's an official-looking letter."

Sinclair took the stairs three at a time and plucked the letter from his mother's outstretched hand. He gazed at it unwilling to open the envelope in case it was a rejection. "Go on Sinclair, open it up," his mother urged, and there it was, a very formal but positive letter stating that he was now a British Overseas Civil Servant in the service of Her Majesty the Queen. Further details revealed that he was being offered a post as a Junior Officer in the Department of Agriculture in Zomba, Nyasaland.

"Come on Mother let's celebrate. How about getting hold of Jeremy and Vicky; a spot of Chinese and a glass of wine in town tonight." Sinclair whirled his Mother off her feet. She was delighted at the thought of having her three children together for an evening. "Hope the twins can get out of lectures at such short notice." Suddenly it was a great day for both of them.

After a few days of almost continuous telephone calls giving the good news to relatives and friends, Sinclair came down to earth. There was so much to be done in eight short weeks. Firstly he was requested by the Colonial Office to attend a medical and briefing the following week and the letter was accompanied by a long list of essential purchases that must be made prior to his expected departure by Union Castle Line on January 15 1955. The list included regulation khaki uniform with shorts to the knee, white formal wear, pith helmet, (which had a question mark beside it) knee stockings, six bathing towels, bedding and personal linen. It reeled on. 'A bit like joining a Victorian boarding school,' Sinclair thought.

However Sinclair's mother also remembered boarding school clothing lists and a glint came into her eye. This was her area of expertise, had she not kitted out two sons for St. Aiden's College and one daughter for St. Mary's Abbey! She rushed for her measuring tape and began taking the most intricate and detailed measurements of her son. "I say steady on Mother, you're not fitting me out for a coffin. What will Aunt Emma say? I thought she was coming today for her weekly lunch and gossip." Sinclair protested but it was no use and that is how Aunt Emma found them as she breezed through the front door looking remarkably fit for her eighty-seven years. Sinclair told her the good news.

"Decadent youngsters of today," she boomed. "Going off to join all those remittance men in Happy Valley." Her massive amber necklace rattled in excitement. "Not Kenya, Aunty dear, I'm going to Nyasaland," murmured Sinclair. "Same thing my boy, all those African countries are the same. It's the hot nights you see." Sinclair gazed at his relative and marvelled at her confident knowledge considering she had never travelled further than Brighton in her entire life.

In fact when he told her he had applied for a post with the Colonial Service in Nyasaland, she said at once she knew the country like the back of her hand. However, he knew that the nearest she had been to Africa was the coconut shy at Hampstead Fair, but, marvel he must at the incredible certainty in which she elaborated on her in-depth knowledge of Nyasaland. "Careful of the head hunters my boy, don't want to have your shrunken topknot decorating the hut of Chief Whatiwhatsit and his forty naked wives." She laughed loudly as she bit into an after-lunch-apple and continued. "Now for heavens' sake don't take up with a concubine otherwise you'll never get a nice local gel to look at you."

Sinclair and his mother exchanged wry looks. Old Aunt Emma was getting even more impossible, in fact rather odd. At the same time Sinclair realised that he would have to be a little cautious on British knowledge of Africa, certainly if Aunty Emma is anything to go by.

The following week, the extraordinary official who briefed him at the

Colonial Office confirmed this opinion. Arthur Hope Huntingdon had been a Colonel in the Indian Army and his main advice to Sinclair was short, sharp and simple.

"Whisky and soda every night dear boy, keeps the old malaria at bay. Throw away the pills, utter rubbish. Does something nasty to your love life you know. Now as to the work side, keep your nose clean when it comes to Civil Service rules. Discipline, discipline is most important, when you are dealing with the locals. Never drink the bloody water, heaven forbid, water is absolutely out, full of you know what." His marble-sharp eyes fastened on Sinclair's face. "Heard about bilharzia? Apparently it's some sort of ghastly worm. Gets up your John Thomas and then wiggles it's way upwards to your brain. It's the locals' fault of course. Always pissing into rivers. Sinclair looked suitably shocked as HH continued. "As soon as you get to Zomba don't forget to sign on at Government House there's a good lad, otherwise the Gov gets narked. Let me see what else."

All the time that he was talking, HH or The Last Warrior, as his colleagues called him affectionately, was searching for further bits of information in file drawers and cupboards. He spied a single sheet written in red under his teacup, blotted off the excess tea and continued. "Ah yes most important, Try not to go bush, there's a good chap. Wash whenever you can, change your shirt and toast the Queen as the sun goes down."

He stood up with his hand outstretched just as an ancient tea-boy came into the room bearing a battered tray on which stood a cracked mug. "Oh! tea-time again. Sorry old chap I can't offer you a cuppa but there's a tea club you see and some of the others get quite ugly if visitors get tea for nothing. Of course, you could donate something to the Christmas Cheer if you're desperate." HH's magnificent moustache quivered with expectation but Sinclair eyed the almost-black murky liquid and hastily declined the offer.

However HH continued to boom away like a Queen's Birthday Parade cannon as he shook hands and skilfully steered Sinclair through piles of files to the door. "Here are just a few forms which must be filled in and sent back to me before you leave Britannia. Quick as possible if you please old lad. I have to complete your file and send it onto your PS in Nyasaland before you board the jolly old Union Castle. Orders from the rajah at the top you know."

"Right ho," said Sinclair, but as he left, a file dated five years previous caught his eye. 'So much for the most efficient Civil Service in the world, I guess I'm safe from in-depth scrutiny for a few years to come,' he murmured to himself, as he joined his mother in Lyons Corner House for tea and buns.

"Talking to yourself already dear, bad sign." Sinclair's mother smiled and covered his hand with hers in a brief moment of affection. "I wish your father had lived to see how well you three children have turned out. I'm going to miss you my son, miss you very much indeed."

Sinclair thought back to childhood memories of his Dad who as a pilot with the RAF was killed flying over Düsseldorf in1941. He gave his mother a brief hug, "You've been wonderful Mother bringing us up on your own. I am sure Dad would have been so proud of you."

There was a brief sad silence until Sinclair said briskly. "Now come on Mum, this is supposed to be a happy day so let's have another cake and celebrate."

It was a good evening and Sinclair slept long and deep next morning. He awoke to the sound of the telephone ringing. "I'll get it Mum." It was Mr Hope Huntingdon. "Forgot to tell you old lad, always wise to read up about the place before you arrive. Makes them feel you care you know. I've popped a few booklets in the post. Read them up there's a good chap. Have a top-hole time on the boat. Cheerio".

Sinclair had no time to utter a word. In fact, old HH could have been talking to the char for all he knew. He told his mother about the call and the shared laughter seemed to warm them both as they marched briskly down to the library.

"Tell you what Mum, I think old HH is a lot brighter and efficient than I thought he was, funny how that generation is always trying to play down the academic streak. I bet he could talk for hours on cricket and polo though. Anyway I think I'll look in the library for some background material on Nyasaland, but let's go to Lucy's Tearoom and have tea and a bun first."

Two days later HH's books arrived and Sinclair was very glad they did. "Mum, I think I am going to really enjoy travelling up through Africa to Nyasaland. I have found out quite a bit and some of it reads like a horror story. Listen to this; it's called 'The Scramble for Africa. In 1884, three European countries, England, France and Germany met in conference in Berlin to discuss how to split up Africa between them. No African representatives were invited.' Can you believe it?"

He raised an eyebrow and looked across at his mother who looked doubtful. "Sounds a bit unbelievable to me. Can't imagine that English people would behave like that." Sinclair looked sharply at his mother. "What about Queen Victoria's Empire Mum? She wasn't called Empress for nothing." Sinclair turned away and looked out of the window to hide his astonishment. 'Had his mother forgotten the long list of countries tied to England from the days of Queen Elizabeth the First and how those ties were imposed!' His mother looked doubtful. "Well Sinclair, I didn't take history in senior school but I can't imagine any English person doing anything unkind or unfair when they go abroad. It's just not our way. Think of your father."

Sinclair knew then at the mention of father it was useless to continue the subject but suddenly he realised that maybe, just maybe, he would not find British rule in Africa all that acceptable. But how could he think that. British justice was honoured worldwide. It was all so confusing. Perhaps it would be best to wait and see.

No words were necessary now, they would have been difficult to find anyway, so he gave her a hug. “Cheer up Mum, just count up all the extra bridge games you can fit in when I leave the family nest.” His mother threw the tea towel at him and the difficult moment passed, but Sinclair pondered upon it later. ‘HH’s opinion, now Mum’s, why do I feel something is not quite right’.

CHAPTER TWO
GOODBYE ENGLAND

The weeks flew by and astonishingly everything fell into place. The bureaucracy turned out to be surprisingly painless and the forms, though complex in composition, were highly orderly. Everything down to the small scar on his left foot was faultlessly recorded.

At last the day of departure arrived. Sinclair stood on Victoria Station waiting to board the boat train. He felt very unwell and for several reasons. Firstly, he had rather over-indulged at his farewell party the previous night and secondly, the vaccination scratches and immunization injections had taken a heavy toll. How much worse would it be to actually have yellow fever, cholera and smallpox, he thought. He wished he could say goodbye to his mother quickly, get on the train and sink into oblivion until he reached Southampton.

"Think I'll get in Mum," said Sinclair giving her a final hug. "I'll write. Don't worry about me, I'll be just fine." His mother gave him a peck on the cheek and thrust a parcel of sandwiches into his pocket, "Your favourites, darling, egg and mayonnaise." Sinclair turned slightly green and tottered to his seat. He closed his eyes but suddenly his dream of peace and sleep was shattered as three boisterous and very healthy young men burst into the carriage. "Hallo old chap, saw from your luggage you are going to Nyasaland. Great, that's where we are going. Joining the Police you know. I'm Peter, he's Henry and that's Alan. OK chaps, what about a spot of arm-wrestling?"

The three looked enquiringly at Sinclair. Sinclair pointed to his bandaged arm. "Sorry fellows, I had a bad do with the rotten jabs." They left him alone initially but because they were very friendly young men they decided to take Sinclair under their wing and he was swept hither and thither, up and down the train to visit other friends and to have a drink, or two or three. Eventually, they were certainly instrumental in helping him up the ship's gangway and taking him down to his bunk in the bowels of the Windsor Castle where he slept and slept and slept.

Suddenly Sinclair awoke with a start. The cabin was dark and the vessel was moving. He crawled off the bunk and peered down the passage just in time to meet head on the full weight of the future Police Force of Nyasaland, who were sharing the 4-berth cabin with him. "Time for grub Sinclair, just came to get you." Sinclair groaned and thought this must be death, but once in the cheerful dining room, he felt surprisingly better. The food was good, the company excellent and as the mists of alcohol displaced his pain, he soon began to realise that this trip was going to be fun. "Cheers, chaps." he said. "Here's to the latest band of unsung heroes. Raise your glasses men to the white-robed saviours of Nyasaland..."

Suddenly, a miserable-looking elderly man, sitting on his own at a nearby table, interrupted Sinclair's speech roughly. "Bloody bunch of idiots. Heroes! Saviours! Do you know what you really are? White ants! You even look like a lot of ruddy insects." He almost choked, but continued. "Wave after wave of you going out to Africa with cucumber sandwiches, old school ties and your bloody accents. You're rooineks, bloody red necks, all of you rushing around in a muddle, writing reports that nobody reads. Jere!" The old man's voice was drowned by a roar of protests from the lads on Sinclair's table. "Steady on there." "What a cad." A couple of the lads started to get up. A fight was in the making and already the news had reached the Captain's table.

A senior steward appeared magically at the table and whispered confidentially. "Don't worry lads, he's a South African trader in Nyasaland; often travels with us. Finds it difficult to get Government contracts, so he can't say anything good about the Civil Service, or the British. Not a bad chap really just a case of sour grapes I think. Gets on well with the locals, speaks their lingo and does quite a lot of trading between Africa and England."

The elderly man sank back into his seat and gazed into his glass. He took no further notice of the bright party of youngsters and as the night wore on there was a great deal of laughter among the young recruits. "Fancy that old bugger calling us white ants! Scorpions perhaps, butterflies, worker bees more like it but not white ants! What an insult!" Sinclair pondered on the situation and thought to himself, 'White ants? Ants are pretty useful little fellows, nippy and orderly. I don't mind being called a white ant but I really wonder why that old fellow had to be so confoundedly awkward.'

Later, much later, as he weaved his way down to Deck E, he was surprised to find the trader sitting on the final flight of stairs. He looked old; he looked ill and a funny colour, almost yellow. "Like a hand Sir." Sinclair inquired. The trader looked up and fleetingly the hatred was there but he grunted "Wouldn't mind a young shoulder to help me to my cabin, my leg's playing up." Sinclair introduced himself as he helped the elderly man to his feet and down the passage to his cabin. "I'm Sinclair Brown, Sir."

The old man stopped for breath and took a long hard look at Sinclair. Was this politeness another English trick, after a veiled insult? But looking at Sinclair's honest young face he decided that there was no immediate threat. "My name's Pieter du Plessis and I'm grateful to you Sinclair Brown. Come in for a last glass before you turn in." The old trader stretched out a hand and almost managed an inviting smile. Sinclair needed a 'last glass' like a hole-in-the-head; in fact, he longed for his bed, but he also knew that this was an important bridge-building invitation and surprisingly, it proved very entertaining.

He soon discovered that Pieter du Plessis had been a big game hunter in his youth. A successful one until a faulty rifle found him fighting for his life with a young leopard in the Zambezi Valley and after months of hospitalisation he was forced to turn to trading for a living. "A life I hate," he confided to Sinclair. "But what wonderful hunting stories you must have to tell," Sinclair said. "Tell you what, come and meet all the boys for a glass tomorrow. I'm sure we could all learn a lot about Africa from you."

"Would you really want to listen to an old Boer's hunting stories?" Pieter was obviously surprised at the suggestion, but he actually smiled at Sinclair's cheery answer. "Of course we would Sir, we Brits are not all bad you know and the Boer War's been over for rather a long time." Sinclair slapped Pieter on the shoulder. "See you tomorrow then. Sleep well," and went off whistling 'God Save the Queen'. 'Ah well,' he thought, 'Hope I've done my bit for inter-cultural relations.'

CHAPTER THREE
ANTS ON HIGH SEAS

'The three-week sea voyage was rather like a trip to Hollywood with dinner at the Ritz thrown in,' Sinclair wrote to his family. *'In fact every night there's a party going on somewhere in the boat,'*

Indeed every meal was a massive offering of diverse dishes, which Sinclair, who had grown up in the war years, had only seen illustrated in his mother's old cookery books. However, after a couple of rather queasy days getting his sea-legs, he and his new-found friends woofed down the smoked salmon and cream cakes with great gusto. *'You'll never believe it Mother dear, he wrote. Every day a seven-course breakfast, with sausages, two eggs, more if you want, masses of bacon and kidneys. It's absolute heaven,'*

'To-morrow we stop at Madeira and we are all getting off to explore the island. I'll try and get you one of those hand-embroidered tablecloths and matching table napkins. I remember you really fancied that set in Harrods,'

'Oh Mum I'm having such fun and if I was really honest, I would like the boat trip to last for ever - but maybe not - I'm also really excited at the possibilities of the new life ahead of me. Fancy me as the next Governor, ha ha! Send my best to the twins. Who knows they may end up out here and you too Mum. Whoops the gong's going for lunch, another meal again. Will I ever tire of smoked salmon? Hope to find a letter from you waiting at Cape Town,'

The days flew by in a dream of laughter and friendship with deck sports and prizes, a hilarious fancy-dress ball and a ship's concert where the lads dressed up as ballet dancers and gave their version of The Dance of the Little Swans. Even the Captain laughed, especially when Sinclair's tutu, fashioned out of toilet paper, unrolled revealing a brightly striped bathing costume. Sinclair heard a roar of laughter and looked quickly towards the audience where he saw Pieter du Plessis sitting with an attractive middle-aged woman. He was obviously enjoying the concert and the company. Sinclair gave him a wave, 'I do hope the old bugger finds a spot of happiness. His stories have been incredible and everyone has enjoyed them.' "Get back into line Sinclair," hissed Henry, "You're ruining the act," Sinclair pulled a hideous face and got an extra cheer from the audience. "Jealousy will get you nowhere old lad," he murmured. "Theatrical experience does reveal itself," The audience enjoyed even more the rough and tumble which took place. A dear old lady knitting away in the corner seat, smiled over her glasses. "What it is to be young,"

Peter surprisingly performed a very competent tap-dance although the roll of the ship did cause him to vanish regularly from the sight of the audience who were tucked under a tarpaulin and wrapped in rugs. "Can't quite understand this dance at all, Ethel," muttered one old man with a moth-eaten handlebar moustache, obviously an ex-Indian Army man. "Why does this idiot keep running off the stage?"

Little did he know that Peter was dicing with death as he bounced left and right off the metal rails of the entertainments-deck. Nevertheless rewards came later as Peter earned many a free drink, as he stripped off to show his bruises, during the all-night party that followed the concert.

Crossing the line was the usual rowdy affair as the lads went through the time-honoured ceremony of being shaved by King Neptune and tipped into the swimming pool. They helped capture the ship's very pretty nurse and cheered like mad when she came out of the pool with her dripping nylon uniform now see-through and clinging to her magnificent body. All the boys immediately fell in love with her but despite some very persuasive moments they did not get very far as she was already engaged to the Chief Purser. "How could she go for such a weedy little runt," muttered Alan.

Desperate and unlikely love affairs, spiced by the limitations of the trip, mushroomed on every deck. Business opportunities were discussed in the many bars and incredible friendships were formed over cups of hot soup at elevenses with addresses exchanged at card-tables and intimate dinners. Sinclair really felt that he could quite comfortably carry on with this lifestyle of floating round the oceans of the world indefinitely until he and his friends climbed up to the deck on the last, slightly chilly, morning to gaze on Cape Town set against the magnificent backdrop of Table Mountain.

"Wow, Africa," they breathed. No other words seemed adequate.

CHAPTER FOUR
ANTS CRAWL UP AFRICA

They were hooked. Their fate was sealed. The latest batch of white ants had arrived and it seemed that Sinclair, Peter, Henry and Alan had already been singled out for specialised treatment because, under normal transport circumstances, most recruits travelled round the Horn and up the East Coast to Portuguese East Africa to gain access to Nyasaland. However, since the rather perilous railway line from Beira to Limbe had been washed away in the recent rains, the group had to face a three-day train journey to Salisbury in Southern Rhodesia and then a drive up a somewhat unknown road through PEA.

Unknown, and in some cases, un-built, according to 'Murky' Waters the gloomy Nyasaland representative in Cape Town. "Don't fancy your chances lads, flooded low-level bridges, lions and then there's the ghastly ferry over the Zambezi River at Tete. Pilot's always drunk." But the boys keen for adventure were ready for everything. "Sounds quite a challenge," said Sinclair cheerfully, "As long we can get a cold beer along the line." "Some chance of that." Murky gave a brief smile. "When I drove up there last year with one of my fishing pals, we counted at least forty miles of nothing between each grass hut!"

Murky enjoyed the look of horror on the boys' faces but then felt rather ashamed at spoiling their obvious excitement on the long and completely unknown journey ahead. He gave Sinclair a friendly punch in the arm. "Never mind lads, after tomorrow, you probably won't see the sea for a couple of years, so go off and enjoy yourselves down at the harbour. You can't visit Cape Town without trying a seafood platter down at the Harbour Café. Sitting under the stars, watching the fishing boats pull in with the lobster you are just about to eat, it's magic." The boys' mouths watered and Murky took advantage. "Tell you what I'll drop you off if you like. Think you can find your way back to the hotel?"

It was a dream of an evening which was made all the more pleasant by some female company when a party of magnificently tanned girls crowded into the next table. One of them was getting married the next day and they were ready for a good party. Within a very short time two of the wooden tables laid out on the quay were pushed together. A memorable evening was about to begin.

The warm evening breeze carried the romantic piped music across the star-filled sky as the smiling waiters presented the succulent platters of freshly cooked seafood and a range of delicious sauces. Even the wine had a champagne quality about it and Sinclair felt a sense of unreality about the evening. It was almost as if he was living out some sort of dream.

"Pity we have to move on so quickly, eh boys," Alan raised his glass to the pretty girls. "I'll never forget this evening." His voice broke and he hid it with a cough and there was a strange almost embarrassed silence.

But ever-practical Sinclair realising that adding romance and a spot of emotion to the present scenario was a touch too much. He decided that it was time to leave. So with many promises of keeping in touch with the girls, the four of them went back to the hotel. But although they were all tired, somehow it was difficult to fall asleep; there were just too many new experiences to think about.

Sinclair gazed out of the hotel window across the moonlit sea and threw the scraps of paper covered with Cape Town addresses into the waste-paper bin. 'Enough is enough,' he said to himself, 'but gosh, it certainly was fun.'

The next day, rather sad at having to leave Cape Town without a really good tour of the ancient city, particularly taking the cable car to the top of Table Mountain, the lads boarded the train at Cape Town station and spent a couple of hot and dusty hours sorting out seats, bedding and meal tickets.

'Not like going to Clapham Junction, Mother dear,' Sinclair wrote as the train chugged laboriously through the African bush. *'We're all covered with a fine red dust and last night at dinner Peter got his soup in his lap when the train came to an abrupt halt. Apparently the guard had left a box of chickens at the last halt and so we went all the way back again. Can you believe it?'*

'It's so strange sleeping in a moving train Mum, a bit like going back to the nursery rocking chair. At every stop, the locals crowd the windows and try to sell carvings, strange fruits and very suspicious-looking cool drinks. We're very fed up with Alan because he bought a huge wooden giraffe, which takes up precious room in the compartment. We made him sleep with it in his bunk as a punishment and it fell out of the window last night but the train was travelling so slowly, Alan was able to hop out and pick it up. Not damaged either. Can you believe that too?'

'Yesterday we travelled up through South Africa and Bechuanaland and crossed the border into Southern Rhodesia. Guess what then? The customs and immigration officials came right onto the train at Plumtree and all the formalities were carried out in a very friendly way as we rocked through the bush.'

'When we reached Bulawayo, the oldest town in Southern Rhodesia, there was enough time to stretch our legs and visit a local hotel for a shower and a

delicious breakfast. It was only 7am but already the sun was hot as we strolled back along the amazingly wide streets. Apparently the width was necessary in the early days, as more and more development took place, to allow the cumbersome ox wagons to turn around in one swing. Sometimes they had as many as 16 oxen pulling one wagon. While we waited to re-board the train we had a chat with the friendly stationmaster. He proudly told us the Bulawayo station platform was the longest in the world and that camels were once used to carry people and goods through Bulawayo. How would you fancy that Mum when you are shopping in Bromley High Street?'

'As the train set off, almost on time, we settled down for a read and a snooze, but quickly became aware of watching eyes, as an endless row of school children side-stepped along the footboard OUTSIDE the carriage. We found out later that it is an old Rhodesian school custom, to celebrate the opening and closing of a school term. Can you imagine old Freddie Cox allowing that to happen on his Dulwich Line? Hold on Mum, lunch gong, I will continue this letter later.'

Two hours later -letter continued. *'Lovely lunch Mum...sort of rice-cottage pie, a bit too much curry for me but very tasty. I think the waiter said it was babootie, something like that anyway. Well, after a snooze, I went back to looking out the window. The train rocked on through seemingly endless, uninhabited bush and savannah peppered with stark granite hills. Occasionally we would surprise a family of baboons searching the tracks for fruit peelings and discarded food from the buffet car, and once or twice saw a massive herd of buffalo grazing peacefully along with zebra and impala,'*

'Now we are coming up to a water point and I can see a group of little children playing an intricate game with stones and markings in the dust. Whoops, the train is slowing down and'...

'O Lordie, monkeys have just jumped onto the roof of the carriage'...

"For heaven's sake close the windows Sinclair - those little rascals will pinch anything they can reach." Peter's shout came too late as Sinclair's pen and notebook disappeared from the carriage seat. With a bellow of rage Sinclair opened the door, jumped out and ran after the little thief who was now fighting with the other monkeys wanting a share of the booty. Sinclair grabbed the pen and leapt back into the train, which had started to move. "Now I understand the meaning of monkey business", he gasped, "Look out Peter, the blighters have pooped on your pillow."

A loud knock on the carriage door interrupted the laughter. It was the guard. "Just to let you know we will be arriving in Salisbury station tomorrow morning at six o'clock lads, so I advise you to get your cases packed before retiring tonight, only a cup of tea and a biscuit to wake you up, I'm afraid, but there are some nice places where you can get a good breakfast, even though it is Sunday."

In fact, quite unexpectedly, the young recruits were met by a pleasant middle-aged couple called John and Lyn Carter, who told them they had just been transferred from Limbe in Nyasaland to Salisbury. "It's the capital of Southern Rhodesia you know. I'm with Imperial Tobacco. I expect you've heard of them. Now let's get you a good breakfast." John Carter spoke rather like a machine gun in full blast and the boys grinned at each other as he led the way to an enormous Chevrolet. "Fancy trying to find parking space for this monster in England," whispered Henry. John caught the words and turned with a wide grin. "Space we have in Africa, boys, and also cheap fuel, one shilling and sixpence a gallon, suit you." What could the boys say but "fantastic".

They went to a comfortable little café in the middle of Salisbury for a 'real English breakfast'. "About three times the size of an English breakfast, actually," murmured Sinclair as the plates were brought to the table, by two elderly white ladies wearing old-fashioned aprons and ankle socks.

Their warm Yorkshire accents were strangely reassuring and their large smiles, encasing enormous china false teeth, suddenly reminded

Sinclair of Aunt Emma. He felt a pang of homesickness. "Stop day-dreaming, Sinclair, and pass the tomato sauce," Henry was anxious to get started on the meal. Suddenly, he looked closely at the sausages, "What are these dark brown ones?" "That's boerwors," said John with a smile. "Not your English porker, but a traditional Afrikaner recipe from South Africa and delicious," and indeed they were. The Carters took the boys for a quick tour of Salisbury, which was a real surprise to the travellers. An ultra-clean City offering just about every modern facility from a spacious shopping area called First Street to a gracious central park, historic government buildings, some interesting pioneer buildings and a couple of old hotels. 'What a pity we have to leave so soon,' Sinclair thought.

Recently, a couple of nightclubs had opened their doors and John reported that they were hoping to import some international cabaret artists for a season. "Well, maybe for a week or so, but apparently they've already written to Petula Clark. Hear they are throwing in a Zambezi Valley trip to have a look at game in the wilds as an extra incentive," said John with a laugh and a wink. "Nothing like facing a charging elephant, especially when you manage to take a photograph to show off when you get back home to England."

Later that day Sinclair, beer in hand, leant back on his chair shaded on the cool Salisbury Sports Club veranda and looked out across the very green grass and magnificent flowering bushes which filled the air with heady perfume. In the distance he saw wide straight avenues lined with magnificent trees and gracious residences.

'I could live in this place,' he thought. 'It's the closest to paradise that I've ever seen.' This opinion was reinforced when they went back to Meikles hotel. "It's like the waiters read your mind," gasped Henry. "I was just thinking about another beer, when there was old Kumwani with his big smile, sparkling tray and another ice-cold beer. Bloody marvellous!"

Before he went to bed, Sinclair decided to finish off his letter home and post it at reception. 'Maybe the post from Nyasaland might be a bit dicey.' Earlier that afternoon someone at the Salisbury Sports Club had been teasing old Henry with stories of the Scarlet Runners, the nickname given to the original Nyasaland postmen. Apparently they were issued with bright red jumpers to wear as they ran through the bush carrying an old-fashioned musket and with a bag of post over their shoulders! Some joker said that only twenty-per-cent of the postmen escaped the claws of the lions that used to sit and wait for them at narrow passes in the hills. Sometimes only scraps of a red jersey identified the unfortunate man's remains and the whereabouts of the abandoned postbag. One Club joker said it sounded as if it should be called The Last Post and everyone laughed but as Sinclair said later 'the awful thing is that it could be true.'

'Dear Mum, letter continued... sorry the last letter finished in a bit of a panic. Now we are in Salisbury, and what a fantastic place. You would love it! It is so clean. Not a scrap of paper in the streets and apparently the fire-engines wash down the roads every week before the town wakes up.'

'We are in the middle of the rainy season and it goes on until about April, but Mum, it's summer and it's so warm. Nothing like our holiday last August in Bognor Regis. Ha ha. They even call them 'the Civil Service rains', very orderly. Apparently the season starts in November each year with a bang and plenty of thunder and lightning. Seems from then on it rains three times a day - going to work, lunchtime and going home time, with plenty of lovely sunshine in between to get the clothes dry! Then Mum, there's the promise of about seven months without rain between May and November. What do you think of that? However, I am a bit worried about the humidity in Nyasaland, but I read somewhere that because Zomba is at the foot of a mountain, we get the odd refreshing shower to cool us off. Hope you get this letter quickly, love to the twins, your loving son, Sinclair.'

CHAPTER FIVE
ANTS ON THE HELL RUN

At 5am the next morning, a smiling waiter, a tray of tea and a packed lunch awakened the boys. Sinclair looked out of the window onto the historic Cecil Square and saw the dawn streak across the sky. He had slept more or less on the spot where the British flag was first raised in 1890. It was a memorable moment but now it was time to leave for the North, 'Unknown Territory', as it was marked on his ancient map of Africa still hanging on his bedroom wall in England. He felt a slight flutter of fear in his stomach. 'Must be indigestion' he thought and took a second cup of tea. 'Mum's remedy for everything.'

Within thirty minutes they were all piling into a rather ancient but sturdy Bedford truck driven by Joseph Phiri, a Nyasa employed by Stansfields of Salisbury who had been running a transport service between the two countries since 1931. "Sorry bosses, only two can sit in the cab with me. The others go in the back. Soon be a nice jolly crowd because I pick up three passengers from Mutoko Hotel, Mr Barney Kaplan sent message. Mutoko very nice hotel, bed, table and chair in every room with a candle and a whole box of matches. Piri piri chicken every night too, very, very nice." Joseph beamed round at the boys but they were at a loss for words. 'What the hell was piri piri chicken anyway and what was so special about a WHOLE box of matches for heaven's sake?'

Soon the luggage was piled onto the roof carrier and, after a certain amount of argument, Sinclair and Peter volunteered to take the first turn in the back of the truck. They climbed under the tarpaulin and sat among the freight. Two simple wooden benches lined the sides of the truck interior, which was lit by a couple of windows protected from flying stones and trees by a fine metal screen. "Won't be able to see much out of these windows," Sinclair grumbled. But Peter, ever practical, said, "Well, at least we'll be protected from dust and bugs Sinclair." However, the boys soon spied some bales of hay and decided that they might be a shade more comfortable as seats. They braced themselves as the vehicle started up and swung out onto the main road north.

"When will we get to Zomba, Joseph?" asked Henry as the three of them squashed into the cab. "We'll get there, Boss, when we get there," was the cryptic reply. "Yes Joseph, but today, tomorrow, next week?" persisted Alan.

Joseph looked rather worried as he thought about how he could explain the perils of the journey without the bwanas refusing to come. "Well, it is something like this. Sometimes it takes me a day, sometimes three days. Once it took me a month, let's see what happens this time. Maybe road closed for repairing, sometimes the ferry is broken, may be the truck breaks down. Then sometimes one of the four border posts is closed down and so we wait for it to open. So I bring can of water and six loaves of bread just in case." Joseph settled himself behind the big wheel. Short in stature and very fat, he was sitting on an old beer crate covered with newspapers, and could just about see the road ahead.

The boys exchanged anxious glances. Just in case what? Why four border posts? "Look at the map lads, there's just miles of nothing. A border post called Mutoko; another called Changara, not far from Tete at the Zambezi River. Then there's, looks like Dzobue...." He peered closely at the map. "Or is it Dzobwe, and finally Mwanza, right up here, ten miles from Blantyre. What on earth are they all guarding?" The four of them bent over Henry's map and watched his finger trace the single line running through seemingly uninhabited country. Not even the security of the occasional village name marked anywhere. Somehow the journey seemed to have taken on a rather more sinister aspect. "Tell you what, Joseph, let's buy a crate of beer, some fruit and biscuits," Henry said firmly. Future events made that a good decision.

In the back of the truck, the bales of hay moved and rolled with every turn of the steering wheel. "I'm starting to get hay fever," Peter groaned and sneezed several times. "Now don't start," growled Sinclair. "Otherwise I'll throw you to the lions." Luckily at that moment, he had no idea how close he was to the possibility of that happening.

However, the travellers soon settled down to enjoy the first leg of the journey that took them through magnificent farming area called Murewa, according to Joseph. The early morning sun lit up tobacco and maize fields stretching as far as the eye could see. "Wouldn't mind being a farmer in this country," commented Sinclair as he peered through a now dust-covered window. "Look at the size of this spread, cattle too. The farmers must all be millionaires but I wonder why they don't do something about the roads. These strips are ghastly,"

But soon the road became a great deal worse as they approached the Rhodesian border post at Mutoko. The edges of the two narrow strips of tarmac, which constituted the main road north, were broken in many places and looked mighty sharp to the boys. "Good Lord, Joseph, can't you go a bit slower, it's so deep between the strips. What happens if your tyres get stuck in that middle rut, it looks so deep?" Alan wiped the sweat off his face and found his handkerchief covered in a ghastly red mud. "Please not to speak those words young Master. Bad luck." Joseph gave an enormous shudder.

“ I guess he must have had a bad accident”, whispered Alan to Henry. Joseph heard, “Too true Boss, it could have been. Big truck came toward me, very fast. Also one wheel stuck in the middle. He just got out in time, if not we all die.” There was a terrible silence as all eyes glued to the road ahead.

But gradually Joseph and the vehicle seemed to settle in a comfortable relationship with the strips and soon eyes began to close. The boys were beginning to feel the early start to the day. They slept for about thirty minutes.

Then suddenly, without any warning, certainly for Sinclair and Peter in the back, the vehicle veered off to the left. They were thrown from one side to the other. Joseph had met up with oncoming traffic, not just one car, but also a whole convoy of army vehicles. The long train of dusty tanks and armoured cars took half an hour to pass them and all that time Joseph struggled to hold his vehicle on the left strip. The grumbles and shouts from the boys in the back of the van grew louder and louder but there was no way in which Joseph could stop. At last, after the final camouflaged army vehicle had passed, Joseph pulled over under a tree. He was exhausted but still managed to smile when the two lads climbed painfully out of the tarpaulin.

“I say Joseph, what the devil do you think you’re doing, we are bruised all over.” Peter had hay in his hair and looked very angry indeed. “Sorry Boss, nothing I could do. There was no room to get off the strips, I did what I had to do.” Joseph looked very tired. Sinclair said very quickly, “Tell you what everyone, let’s take a break, share our lunch packs and have a drink.”

Miraculously, the cool drinks were still cold and after a few quick exercises to stretch sore muscles Henry said, “Come on everyone, we’ve got to get on, our turn in the back Alan,” Joseph went round the back and showed Henry and Alan how to pull the hay bales apart and spread the sweet-smelling dried grass around the sides of the canopy. He advised, "Put on your coats to save your elbows. Sorry young masters, road very bad from now on. Try to sleep a little now."

Surprisingly, they did until the sturdy vehicle slowed down to a crawl to drive through a small village. In the far distance they could see massive pink-coloured hills of solid granite. Henry awoke and caught a glimpse of the lovely view through a hole in the canopy and shouted to Joseph, asking if they could stop and take photographs. But strangely enough, Joseph shook his head vigorously and even seemed to get an extra spurt of energy out of the engine. "No Boss, no stop here. Everywhere in Mutoko is the place of the spirits. We must not anger the spirits. Do not look too strongly at the hills and do not say any rude words about this place, otherwise we will suffer." Joseph seemed to be under heavy emotional stress. Perspiration was pouring down his face as he followed a very ancient old car through the narrow pass that opened out onto a massive plain.

"Looks rather like a moonscape!" gasped Alan as the sun astonishingly lit up the smooth summits of a dozen or so enormous granite hills. Whether the spirits did not like the word moonscape or whether it was just plain bad luck, the old vehicle travelling in front of them suddenly swerved across the road and crashed into a deep ditch.

Joseph and the lads piled out of the truck and helped push the ancient Ford out of the ditch. Astonishingly, the driver was not badly hurt, just a small cut on his forehead. He climbed out of the window with the most enormous smile on his face. "Thanks young bosses. Always take window glass out when I go this road. Road very bad, glass too expensive."

"Somewhere in that statement there's logic," Sinclair murmured as Lancelot Chipembere went round introducing himself and shaking everyone by the hand. "That's a fine name, Lancelot." Henry said.

Lancelot beamed, "Very true boss, my mother chose it from a booku her madam used to buy every week. Something about a mad white man who won a war with a panga, but Chipembere is a big name in Nyasaland. Chief is very fat, his wives very fat, his peoples very fat. Some have plenty money."

There was silence. Nobody knew what to say. Why was Lancelot driving such an old vehicle if the Chipemberes were so rich and why are they all fat?

Joseph came out from under the car where he was assessing the damage. "How can we help Lancelot, Joseph?" Henry, ever practical, broke the awkward pause.

"Easy done, young Sirs. We change burst tyre now. Then when we get to Mutoko down the road, Mr Kaplan, very nice man owning hotel, will lend us a rope to tie up the cracked axle. Then Mr Chipembere can safely get home to Blantyre." Joseph looked surprisingly cheerful "Not too much trouble." He whistled as he jacked up the car and helped change the burnt shreds of the original tyre. "The replacement's not much better." Sinclair murmured. But on it went.

"Don't fancy travelling a couple of hundred miles on a cracked axle, Lancelot. Will you be OK?" Peter did not know that much about the problem but it sounded serious. "Very fine young master, you be behind me all time to help other troubles." Lancelot cheerfully climbed into his battered vehicle.

The boys looked at each other in horror. This was why Joseph was so reluctant to say how long the journey would take. Were they going to have to travel a further three hundred odd miles following a damaged axle? Was it possible? It seemed there was no alternative. Rounding a bend they came upon a barrier across the road. A sign read:

MUTOKO - SOUTHERN RHODESIA
DEPARTMENT OF CUSTOMS AND IMMIGRATION

They had arrived at the Rhodesian border post. The white-uniformed officials were very pleasant and efficient and asked the boys to come in for a cup of tea, but Joseph said "No Bwanas, very sorry must get off, big journey."

"What a shame." Peter whispered to Sinclair as they set off again. " I would really have liked to have a wash and brush up. Did you see that lovely cool office, big fan and a flush toilet too, must be heaven." Sinclair looked uncertain. "Umm I don't know about heaven, being stuck out here in the middle of nowhere is not my idea of the good life, all this heat and dust." They both pondered on the situation. Would they end up in a similar situation when they arrived in Nyasaland!

However, once they reached Mutoko Hotel as Sinclair said, it was like taking a quick tranquiliser. Barney Kaplan turned out to be a charming and gracious host and knew so many interesting stories about the country's development and particularly the old road. He warned them that after leaving Mutoko the dreaded strip road would peter out into plain old Mother Earth and potholes aplenty. But the boys roar, after a cool wash and an even cooler beer on the front veranda, they felt very relaxed. In fact, they were almost dozing when they heard a vehicle approaching. Was it Joseph returning? But no, a car stopped and two adults and a young lad were dropped off at the hotel entrance. It was time to meet their fellow Nyasaland travellers, Frank and Joy Wilson and their teenage son. Jon, a boarder at St. George's College in Salisbury had had an emergency appendix operation in St Anne's Hospital and his parents had rushed down from Zomba, to pick him up and take him to convalesce at home. They had been staying a few days with Frank's brother on a farm in nearby Murewa before going on home.

"Sure you're OK for this rough journey Jon?" asked Sinclair

anxiously. But the family seemed quite relaxed, although Frank said with a rather grim smile, "We actually came down to Salisbury to pick him up in our faithful old 1948 Vauxhall but we've had to leave her in Salisbury for multiple repairs. This road can be very hard on an old vehicle, but we were anxious about Jon and so probably took the journey too fast for the poor old lady." "Quite understandable Sir", said Peter, but he thought to himself 'so some whites are not all that rich?'

Suddenly, they heard drums and, to the boys' amazement, a line of waiters each wearing a long white garment topped with a red fez, undulated out of the hotel front door. They were singing some sort of song that incorporated many different versions of the word 'welcome' and each one of them was beating a drum in a series of complicated rhythms. The boys were mesmerised. Suddenly the drums stopped. The waiters bowed and the headwaiter, in front and a little taller than the rest, roared out. "Lunch is served, Masters and Madam". "Good Lord," gasped Alan, "Is lunch always like this in Africa?" The Wilsons laughed and Joy said, "You'll find that all Africans have a natural talent for the theatrical. They sing and dance magnificently too. Just wait until you get to Nyasaland. Now don't let the food spoil, let's eat."

The boys could not believe the amount of food that awaited them on the back veranda. Massive platters filled with a dozen or more pieces of chicken. Large dishes brimming with rice and extra gravy and colourful salads dotted the long trestle table. "Good heavens, how many people are coming and what's that sort of yellow semolina?" Peter could hardly believe his eyes. "I wish we hadn't filled up on those lunch packs." "Well," said John with a grin, "You can always ask Barny for a doggie bag; in fact that might be a wise thing to do for the journey ahead." Watching from the kitchen door, Barny smiled and nodded his head. He really liked having a lively party at the hotel.

Everyone sat down and there was silence at the boys took their first taste of piri piri chicken. "More than bloody marvellous," said Peter. "Much nicer than curried chicken, but what are you doing with that yellow semolina Jon?" "Not semolina Peter, but sadza, that's what it's called in Rhodesia, and it's yummy." Jon rubbed his stomach in anticipation and carried his piled-up plate to the table.

Frank sat beside Peter and enlarged on the story of sadza. "Actually Peter, what Jon did not tell you is that sadza is the most important every day food throughout Africa. You must have seen the enormous fields of maize growing in the fields a few miles back towards Salisbury?" All the boys nodded in agreement. "Bloody marvellous sight too, all those big cobs," said Sinclair.

Frank took a long pull at his beer, 'Thirsty work educating these new boys' he thought to himself as he continued. "Too true Sinclair, but we call those big cobs, mealies, and the ones you saw were being grown commercially. They are sold to the millers who process them into mealie meal. A local flour if you like. But although the villagers survived on traditional wild cereals before the white farms were established, now they are being given seed to grow this new high quality maize. However, the poor old village mum still has to harvest the cobs, dry them in the sun and then store them away in a secure grass hut. But her real work starts when she pulls out enough cobs to feed her family each day. Now she has to strip the pips, pound them into flour in a traditional wooden pestle and mortar and then cook the meal into a sort of porridge. Despite their repetitive daily tasks, the village women are always smiling and turn each chore into a happy occasion. You should hear them singing as they pound away at the hard pips! But there's a real art to cooking sadza you know and Joy still struggles, don't you dear?"

Joy pulled a face at her husband and picked up the story. "Sadza, called ncema in Nyasaland, sort of takes the place of bread and you can use it to mop up gravy. Remember there is not much cutlery in village life, or in the bush, so this is how we Africans, black and white, use sadza." She smiled at the boys, spooned out a scoop of sadza and, rolling it into a ball in the palm of her hand, she dipped it into her chicken gravy and popped the whole thing into her mouth. "Delicious," she said, closing her eyes in appreciation of the taste.

"I'll have a try," said Peter, and try he did but rolling the sadza and scooping up the gravy was not easy and, when Sinclair jogged his elbow by mistake, the ball flew out of his hand and rolled under the table. There was a united "eeee aaaah" from the waiters who were bewildered by the sudden laughter from all the diners. They were even more amazed at the loud cheers that greeted an enormous fruit salad presented with great ceremony at the end of the meal. "Who would believe we would find the Ritz in the middle of Africa," murmured Henry. "Too bloody true and I would like to stay here for a couple of months," said Sinclair.

But just then Joseph came down the road in the truck and spoilt the magic. "Time to go everyone," he said, looking at the ruins of the lunch on the table. "How did you get on with Lancelot's car Joseph? Have you had something to eat?". Sinclair also realised that the day was slipping by and there were still many miles to go. However, Joseph assured them that he and Lancelot had enjoyed a massive dish of sadza and something he called 'relish' in a local bar before roping up the cracked axle.

Finally Joseph stood up on the running board and shouted, "Please to get in the truck." He seemed to wobble slightly. "Had a couple of beers too by the smell of it," whispered Alan. "Who could blame them?" whispered back Sinclair fiercely. "We had three or four I seem to remember."

Joseph had met the Wilsons before and so as soon as their luggage was loaded, they said goodbye to Barny and staff and with much huffing and puffing all the boys climbed into the back of the truck. It was understood without actually saying it that the Wilsons would travel in front with Joseph.

"O dear God, look at that road ahead, it looks like a ploughed field," gasped Peter. "What are all those ridges, no wonder you say it will be a rough ride Frank?" "Cheer up my lad, those ridges are called corrugations, waves of dried mud really. Buses and heavy lorries create them in the rainy season when we have torrential rains and fierce sun. The mud banks up and the sun bakes it. However, once a year the Governments of all three countries grade their section of the roads, well, they are supposed to. If you are lucky you get a reasonable ride, but not today, the road looks really bad. It's going to be an uncomfortable journey. Hope you are going to be alright Jon?" Frank turned to his son who already looked rather pale. "I'll be OK Dad." There was a silence and each passenger considered the miles ahead. Ominous. "Never mind, cheer up everyone, it's only a hundred and eighty five miles until we hit the tar at Chileka airport."

Joy threw her hat at him. "This is where I go to sleep," she said with a smile. "Want another pain-killer Jon?" The four boys in the back settled down to a card game. The miles and hours went by.

The vehicle toiled up a hill, which took a sharp turn to the right. "Heavens Joseph, how are you going to go down there?" Frank asked as he looked in fascination at the steep winding road ahead and peppered with small boulders. "Only one way," muttered Joseph and swung the wheel over. The vehicle plunged into the bush running along side the roadway. Thorn trees tore at the tarpaulin and boulders scraped the paintwork. Joy covered her eyes and Jon gave a whimper of pain.

Meanwhile in the back the boys had no idea what was happening. Through the flap they could see flashes of bush at crazy angles. "Well lads I guess we are out of control. Heads down and wait for the crash." Henry looked pale. The four boys crouched together arms over their heads.

Suddenly they felt the vehicle slew to the left and miraculously they were back on the road again. There was a strong smell of burning rubber. Everyone jumped out of the truck to check the damage and Joseph disappeared under the bonnet to check the engine. Miraculously, it seemed only the bodywork had suffered where obstacles in the truck's path scored deeply into the paintwork. "Soon get that fixed in Blantyre," said Joseph with a grin.

We're OK," shouted Alan, "Well done, bloody marvellous driving Joseph." Joy started to cry. "Come on old girl, we've been through worse than that," Frank gave her a hug and turned to his son. "How is it my boy?" Jon gave a big smile "Gosh Dad wait until I tell everyone in the dorm what happened." Joseph watched them wondering if they knew how close to death they were. "OK everyone, a quick drink and then back in the van. We still have a long way to go."

Just before they reached the Changara border post, some sixty-three miles before Tete and the Zambezi River, a rather longer stop for refreshments and a leg-stretch was broken by the sudden appearance of a pride of lions. "My God they look hungry," gasped Sinclair as they all sprinted for the truck. Hungry the lions were indeed and quite determined to play a waiting game as they flopped down round the truck, eyes fixed unblinkingly on the sweating occupants in the cab. One young lioness actually stood up and tried to get through the back tarpaulin, which Peter had luckily tied up from the inside. They heard the persistent scratching as claws tore at the rather ancient canvas. Sinclair and Peter crouched in the one corner of the truck, Henry and Alan in the other. They all had their coats over their heads. "I guess this is where we start praying lads," Sinclair said softly. He put an arm round Peter who was visibly shaking. "Bear up old lad, Dover's in sight!" "I don't want bloody Dover and high cliffs, Sinclair, I hate lions but I'm bloody frightened of heights too." Peter spat out at Sinclair and then they all started to giggle. It turned to laughter and finally almost hysterics. Joseph, Frank, Joy and Jon all hissed "Shush," through the broken window between the front cab and the boys, but it was no use, the laughter went on and on and seemingly it frightened off the intruder. At least the scratching stopped.

"Joseph, what can we do?" Peter whispered fearfully. "We wait Boss, we near Portuguese help". Joseph replied as he prepared to settle down for a sleep. And wait they did, for four hours in fact, until suddenly an ancient Land Rover bearing four soldiers came roaring down the dusty road. The soldiers let off a few rounds from very ancient-looking rifles and the lions moved off in rather a stately fashion. Almost as if they were in league with the soldiers Sinclair thought. Saved the boys were, but for an exacting price because the soldiers demanded rescue payment in cigarettes, a loaf of bread and one beer each. "Well death by starvation is infinitely more attractive than death by slow suffocation or being eaten by a lion." Henry muttered, as they set off once more towards the river.

The truck crashed and bumped its torturous way over corrugations covered with thick slimy mud. The lads groaned as the vehicle slithered in all directions but Joseph seemed indifferent to the discomfort. "He's got a lot more fat on his posterior than we have, that's what," whispered Peter. "How I wish I could sleep." Everyone was exhausted, but strangely Joseph remained alert. He was humming a strange repetitive tune. "Almost hypnotic," thought Sinclair, and indeed it was. Soon merciful sleep overtook them all.

CHAPTER SIX
CROSSING THE ZAMBEZI

All the passengers were dozing in uncomfortable knots in the vehicle when the loud hooting of the truck's awakened them with a fright. "What's wrong now, Joseph," muttered Sinclair. "Changara border post young bosses, please to get passports ready, we are about to go into PEA, that's Portuguese land in Africa." Joseph hopped out of the truck and did not seem surprised that the station appeared to be closed and that even though it was mid-morning not a single official was in sight. He went round the back of the building to investigate and the passengers climbed out of the truck and followed him, taking the opportunity to stretch their cramped limbs. Joseph disappeared through a backdoor festooned with empty demijohns of Portuguese wine and soon a great deal of shouting could be heard. After quite a long while, Joseph reappeared looking flustered.

"Big party last night, all still sleeping. We must wait." Joseph reported back after checking the living quarters. "Nonsense Joseph, wake them up man." Henry roared at Joseph. "We've got to get on."

The waking up process was long and noisy and at least one hour was wasted whilst stamps and pads were found and applied liberally to every passport as bleary eyed officials tried to match up photographs with faces. "Are you this one?" "No I am not that one." "Is this you?" " Yes I am that one." "This is like something out of Gilbert and

Sullivan," muttered Sinclair. "Next thing they'll be singing, 'Three little maids are we' and if we are not careful they are going to completely fill up our passports with those ghastly stamps!"

The boys laughed, and then everyone laughed, and amid a great deal of backslapping and handshaking, they were all invited to enjoy a glass of wine or cordial before journeying on. "It seems that everything is done with a great deal of laughter in Africa," said Sinclair thoughtfully. Joseph wiped his sweaty face with what looked suspiciously like a large pair of old pink knickers. "Too true young master, we Africans like to laugh too much."

Eventually everyone piled back into the vehicle. It was another sixty-three miles to Tete and one by one they fell asleep. The loud hooting of the car horn again woke them from an uncomfortable doze. "Now what Joseph," said Alan, very angry at being woken up? "Look young bosses, it is the City of Tete and the Zambezi River." Joseph pointed proudly to the cluster of brightly painted houses surrounding a massive fort. In the distance they saw an enormous stretch of water racing downstream. Nearby a large paddle steamer was tied up to an old tree stump sticking out of the river. They could not make out the namc. "Shades of the deep South riverboats and gamblers," commented Peter, "Wonder if it still works." "Boat very old," said Joseph proudly. "It used to bring machinery up from the sea before roads were made."

"The boat does still operate and Tete is one of the earliest Portuguese communities in this part of Africa," commented Frank. "There's an even better paddle steamer tied up at Chiromo on the Shire River. It's called The Empress, after Queen Victoria of course."

THE EMPRESS PADDLE STEAMER *The Empress was named after Queen Victoria and this paddle steamer was commissioned to open up the water gateway to the country before 1889. Equipment and machinery brought by ship to the East Coast would travel up the Zambezi River and be offloaded onto The Empress for transportation to Chiromo on the shores of the Shire River.*

"Heavens above, that fort looks just like the one in my old nursery." Sinclair swung round to gaze at the stretch of water in front of them. "That river must be a half a mile wide. Are you sure there's no bridge Joseph?" "No bridge, Nkosi, but a modern ferry. I call the pilot again." Joseph went back to the truck and again hooted the horn vigorously.

At first the lads took no notice of what appeared to be a few old planks drifting towards the steep and muddy embankment. Then, to their horror, they saw that the planks formed a sort of wooden platform that was being pulled through the water by a very small and ancient motorboat. The pilot waved a bottle, smiled, showing very white teeth and shouted non-stop incomprehensible instructions to his workers on the ferry and the bank of the river.

Joseph turned to the group. "Back into the truck young masters, the pilot wants us to drive along the causeway to board ferry. The rains have been too good this year and have covered the road. We must be very careful." Then the boys saw that below the level of the racing waters a very narrow muddy causeway covered with rough rocks reached out towards the ferry.

"No room for error on that road," gasped Peter, "and God help us if we go off the side of that ferry, we'll end up down at the seaside." "Don't worry," smiled Joy. "Every time I come to this part of the journey, I just close my eyes from now on until we get off the other side." "Good idea Joy...heavens! You call it a ferry! It's a raft and there's only a two-inch edging between the passengers and eternity. Good heavens those planks seem to be balanced on a whole lot of empty drums." Henry's keen eyes had picked up the awful details. "That pilot's as drunk as a coot too."

A TYPICAL AFRICAN FERRY circa 1950
More like a raft, this one is loaded with vehicles, people and animals.

By now a furniture van, three more cars, assorted bicycles and about twenty pedestrians with goats, chickens and vegetables were queuing behind them to board the ferry. Joseph paid the fee. There was no turning round or turning back. Forward they had to go.

"Maybe this is the time to break out the beers. A bit of Dutch courage is needed here." Sinclair handed out beers as the vehicle sloshed into the water and bounced onto the planks and, whether it was the effect of alcohol on an empty stomach or the sweltering heat of 140 degrees, somehow getting off the ferry on the far side of the river seemed less important than immediate survival to the boys.

After an hour or more during which the pilot shouted conflicting orders to everyone, eventually all the vehicles and people boarded the raft that was tied to the motorboat by a long chain.

"Good Lord," breathed Peter. "He's going to pull us up-stream and then let us drift across to the other side. Looks like a bit hit and miss to me." As he spoke there was a loud grinding sound as the raft stuck on a sandbar beneath the fast flowing river. Shouts and cries heralded the loss of several goats and one dog overboard. The boys watched in fascination as all the animals swam hopelessly for the nearest bank, which was covered with waiting crocodiles.

The pilot shouted angrily. Joseph muttered, "He wants us to start up our engine and rock the truck until we float the ferry off the sandbank. Very dangerous young sirs, please be kind enough to hold on. Once the ferry chain broke and everyone floated sixty miles down river. Ferryman make very bad mistake. Two people fell into the river and were eaten by crocodiles, too terrible."

"I say chaps, we ought to have been paid danger money for travelling this route. I'm going to write to my MP about the whole journey when we get to Zomba!" Henry's face was bright red with sunburn and anger.

"What do you mean WHEN we get to Zomba, I'd say it's IF we get to Zomba!" Peter clung onto Joseph's truck as the ferry floated off the sandbar and approached the far bank where a narrow, steep and very muddy track cut through the riverbank.

"How the hell do we get off the ferry, Frank? Surely the ferry's too high above the ground and anyway all the vehicles are facing the wrong way." Alan was puzzled. "I'll let Joseph tell you," grinned Frank. "Very easy young boss, we use planks and drive down backwards." Joseph grinned as two warped and narrow planks were balanced against the side of the ferry at an angle of forty-five degrees. The boys watched in horror as people, animals, and vehicles tottered down the bouncing planks.

Peter looked at his friends. "Well I don't know about you lads, but I'm taking a chance with walking the plank rather than driving down backwards with Joseph. Last one's a monkey!" The boys ran for terra firma and once safely on land they sat on the baking hot sand and celebrated their survival with a second beer.

"I guess we'll remember to-day for ever," said Peter. "I feel a bit emotional lads, stiffen the sinews and all that. Remember we've still got to go through two more border posts and miles of completely unoccupied territory."

But in fact the onward journey was tame by comparison to the crossing. Dzobwe border post was in the middle of nowhere and, by the time they arrived at Mwanza, they were all too exhausted to do more than lean against the counter under a ceiling fan and hand in the passports, now almost filled with stamps. "I have never ever been so tired in the whole of my life," moaned Alan. There was a murmur of agreement but then Sinclair said, "You know chaps I've been thinking old Joseph does this ghastly journey over and over again, he really deserves a medal so how about a whip round for him." Everyone agreed and only the Wilsons expected the fantastic dance of gratitude. Joseph leapt and whirled and whistled, clapping his hands as he executed a wild traditional dance. "You'd think we had given him a hundred pounds not £4.15," whispered Peter. "It's the thought that counts," said Joy gently.

After dropping off the Wilson family at their home in Zomba, with many promises of meeting up in the future, it was just on ten o'clock when the boys arrived at the Government Hostel in Zomba. The building appeared to be in complete darkness.

They rang a large bell hanging at the side of the large door and waited for what seemed to be ages before they noticed a tiny light travelling along a nearby veranda. Soon a flickering candle appeared followed by a very cross-looking man with a massive moustache. He was also holding a balloon glass and had obviously been enjoying a late night brandy. "What the devil do you think you're doing disturbing me up at this hour?" The boys could smell the after-dinner brandy on his breath.

"Sorry Sir," said Henry crisply, "But we've being travelling from Salisbury since six o'clock this morning, nearly four hundred miles of the most ghastly roads ever travelled and we are hot, tired and very hungry."

"Good Lord man, do you mean to say you are the new recruits? Sorry lads, please come in." The man, who was already in his dressing gown, seemed to thaw out a little when he took a second look at their tired faces. He gestured the lads into a large comfortable sitting room and they collapsed into some well-used chairs.

"Sorry to be so short with you but we expected you tomorrow lads. Of course by rights you Police recruits should go straight to the Police Camp but it's too late tonight. Tomorrow's another day. My name's Andy Anderson by the way, I'm the Hostel Sperintendent. Now let's see what we can rustle up in the way of a meal. Nothing cooked mind, the Governor had a big party this evening and so as usual we all had to give up our electricity tonight. Will cheese and pickles do?"

"Why do you have to give up your power supply if the Governor has a party Sir," Sinclair asked curiously. " Not Sir, old man, Andy will do. About the electricity, very simple really, the supply to the whole town is inadequate so if and when H.E. has visitors, we have to get out the candles and have a cold supper." The boys looked at each other. It didn't seem to worry Andy.

A couple of hours later after a delicious snack and cool shower, Sinclair lay between cool sheets under a massive mosquito net spread over a square metal frame somehow attached to his bed. He could smell a really heady perfume floating in through the window. 'Smells a bit like jasmine, wonder if I should shut the window, leopards! snakes! scorpions! he thought sleepily. Gradually, very gradually, he drifted off to sleep to the sound of a pair of owls hooting in the monkey-puzzle tree. 'Well, I've made it this far, mother dear, but what will to-morrow bring I wonder,'

CHAPTER SEVEN
WHITE ANTS SIGN ON

Before they all went to bed, Andy suggested that they sleep in and generally settle before reporting for duty. "I'll pick you up at ten sharp, Brown, and get you Bobbies collected and taken down to your Camp after breakers. Is that OK with you all?" The boys nodded gratefully. It would be great to have a lie-in after that torturous journey.

Sinclair awoke in the middle of the night to what sounded like the start of a riot. Machine guns seemed to be blazing away until he realised, from the ceiling leaks obligingly dropping into a variety of enamel bowls placed round the room, that it was rain pounding onto the iron roof. 'Heaven's above' he thought, 'will I ever get to sleep again?' But sleep he did, and after breakfasting on a strange sort of melon called paw paw, cereal and delicious eggs and bacon, Sinclair saw that the rain had stopped. Indeed the sun was shining brightly and all the roads were swirling with mist as the fierce sun sucked back the rain and turned it into steam.

"You know Mr Anderson, if it wasn't for the sun and the heat I could be on the Yorkshire moors." Andy roared with laughter. "Call me Andy by the way, I told you that last night, but you know there'll be times lad when you'll be longing for the Yorkshire chills, especially if they put you in charge of the Chikwawa Valley project. They often put new chaps in sweaty places, sort of a character test you see."

Sinclair tried to draw out a few more details of the Valley project but Andy clammed up. "You'll find out my boy, but don't worry, first time they'll send a good chap with you. Not bad if you get a Lakeshore posting though. You start work at six in the morning, hour and a half for breakfast and you finish work at two. Then it's fishing and swimming 'til sundowners." "Sounds great," said Sinclair weakly, "Where's the catch?" But Andy was determined to give him the Thomas Cook tour treatment and skilfully avoided giving Sinclair further information. 'The lad will find out the distaff side soon enough,' he thought.

Sinclair waved good-bye to Peter, Henry and Alan as they drove off to the Police Camp. "Let's meet up again soon," he called out but Andy told him with a laugh "Those chaps will be fully occupied on a training programme for at least three months and they have their own Police Club, a good watering hole actually. Strange thing is though we each keep to our own patch of land. Still I am sure you'll meet them at the Gymkhana Club functions."

Sinclair felt a sudden sense of loss. He had been through so much with his friends and was determined to keep up the connection despite the well-established customs of the British community. 'Damned if I'll let the friendship go.' he thought determinedly, but something at the back of his mind warned him not to openly buck the system. He'd leave contact for a bit.

"Would you like a quick tour of Zomba before the official stuff?" Andy offered. "That would be great," replied Sinclair, rather glad to put off, albeit briefly, the official welcome at the Secretariat and the signing in at the Governor's Lodge.

Zomba, the tiny capital city of Nyasaland appeared to be balanced on the side of a steep mountain and the tour seemed to take less than thirty minutes. They drove down a main road lined with trees and bright trailing bushes. "Look at those beautiful bougainvillea bushes, imported of course, but they simply love the dry hot climate of this country," Andy waved his hand. "Grow anywhere, go green if they are over-watered."

Sinclair spied a couple of discreet shops, two churches and Andy pointed out the police and army camps, a large prison and the top and the bottom hospitals, "I'll explain about that later," said Andy. Various side roads seemed to lead to residential areas. It was very quiet. No pedestrians, no cars, no bicycles. "Where is everyone?" asked Sinclair "Is it a holiday or something?" Andy laughed. "Everyone is at work Sinclair, they are either a working member of the great Colonial Civil Service, kids in school, mums playing bridge or tennis and the servants making the beds. Wait until Saturday morning though."

A quick turn down the hill to the left revealed a massive market where many vendors sat behind small piles of colourful fruit and vegetables. Sinclair could see some tiny eggs, clay pots and a profusion of woven baskets and hats. "Mangoes two a penny, eggs a penny each and lovely cheap beef here," murmured Andy as he pointed towards a carcass of beef hung under a tree. It was covered with flies, which were being swiped, in a rhythmic sort of way and quite ineffectively by a couple of toddlers waving branches of bamboo. 'Enough to turn one into a vegetarian,' thought Sinclair.

"Bit bewildering eh Sinclair?" Andy Anderson gave a grin as his old Vauxhall toiled up a very steep hill to Old Naisi, a new Government residential area filled with modest bungalows. "We call these houses Blackwood Boxes after Michael Blackwood, the man who designed them. O.K I suppose, but a bit ghastly new-town-in-Britain, don't you think?"

OLD NAISI:
Naisi, a Government housing suburb in Zomba.

Sinclair looked at the neat homes and developed gardens and thought 'I bet a lot of young couples in Britain would be thrilled with one of those houses'. By now, they were going down Old Naisi Hill and it was quite evident that the car brakes were poor. Both of them were sweating heavily by the time they reached the bottom road. "Must get something done about these brakes," Andy mused. 'Too bloody right,' thought Sinclair.

Andy wiped his brow and continued with his tour commentary. "But don't worry Sinclair, you can't get lost in Zomba. Only one main road runs through the township. By the way, if and when you ever get married, you would have to move out of the Hostel; I expect you realise looking round the breakfast table to day that the Hostel is really only for visitors and singles. One day you will probably end up with a smallish house at the bottom of the mountain, most likely somewhere in this area."

He pointed towards some rather old depressed-looking houses surrounded by nondescript vegetation. "The suburb is called Misere

Farm but the junior staff who live there call it Misery Farm, shame really. I started off there. It's OK, nice fruit trees but not much of a breeze though." Indeed it was hot, very hot indeed and Sinclair felt his shirt sticking to his back.

Andy went on to explain further. "You see the higher you go up the promotion ladder in the Service, the higher up the mountain you live. The cooler the air! It's quite simple really. A series of rewards, do you get it? But tell you what, I'll take you for a drink at the

ZOMBA PLATEAU, LOOKING TOWARDS QUEEN'S VIEW:
In 1960 Her Majesty Queen Elizabeth, the Queen Mother opened this site which she remarked was 'breathtakingly beautiful'.

Gymkhana Club this evening and when I get home I'll ask the Missus to arrange a picnic for the weekend and we'll take you up Zomba mountain."

He changed gears rather noisily as they began to climb up the plateau above Zomba. "Bit of a tricky road up though, in fact it's so narrow and dangerous that you have to travel up between the hour and half past and down from half-past to the next hour. There's a sort of clock top and bottom of the road. Of course, sometimes after people party at the Ku Chawe Inn and have a few too many glasses they forget about the clock and cars meet nose to nose on one of the narrow bends in the road. Bit nasty of course. Usually the least inebriated driver offers to reverse. Believe it or not, although a few people have gone over the edge no one has actually been killed. Miraculous really." Sinclair felt a sudden pang of fear in his stomach. He wondered how he could bring up the fact that he

TROUT-BREEDING PONDS ON THE SUMMIT OF ZOMBA MOUNTAIN:
During the hot season, a great many residents of Zomba used to brave the perilously narrow road clinging to the side of the mountain, to reach the refreshingly cool climate on the summit.

really wasn't very good with heights, but Andy continued, "It's wonderful up there Sinclair, Trout streams, cool breezes, cottages you can hire if you get to know the right people. Then there's Ku Chawe Inn, a rare old pub perched on the edge of a thousand foot drop. We'll go in for a pint after the picnic. Are you on?"

"Sounds great," Sinclair replied weakly wiping his perspiring face. "Is it always as hot as this?" "It's not the heat old lad it's the humidity, ninety percent humidity at this time of the year. As soon as the rains start we all start to swelter but one gets used to it," Indeed, Andy Anderson looked as crisp as when they had first set out. Wonder how he does it thought Sinclair.

Almost as if he was reading Sinclair thoughts, Andy said "The trick is to drink large amounts of liquid in the cool of the evening, gin, brandy, beer whatever, but never water, don't want a gippy tummy do you. Never drink the water out of the Lake either, it's full of mica." 'Shades of old HH in London', thought Sinclair but the prospects of a regular evening drink in the cool of the Gymkhana Club was enticing. "Roll on four pip emmer, Sinclair." Andy's RAF background came to the fore as he gave Sinclair a friendly slap on the back as they entered the Secretariat. As soon as they went through the double doors there was an immediate sense of order, almost a sort of church-like serenity in fact. Four ceiling fans were quietly spinning at full blast.

"This is the five-star working area Sinclair. When you get to work in these offices, you know you're most likely in line for a gong in some future New Year's Honours List. Hope you're not too disappointed when you see your office. I'll pick you up in an hour's time and take you to Government House." Andy went off whistling Land of Hope and Glory. Later he told Sinclair the Secretariat always had that affect on him. "Sort of brings out the Union Jack in me you see." Sinclair understood completely.

Soon Sinclair was caught up in the intricacies of signing on and settling in. A bewildering parade of faces and names and offices but in general the welcome was genuine and cordial. Later as Sinclair, dressed in his new uniform, rather self-consciously wrote his name and new employment designation in the Governor's book. Andy warned him. "Sinclair, always remember to sign out when you go on leave and sign in when you return. Protocol you know. But also it means you get invited to one of H.E.'s receptions. Rather a bun-fight though and as a matter of fact no one has ever managed to get more than two drinks at any session. I believe the Dept. of Works has kept a betting book on that for years. Still I don't want to put you off." Sinclair looked up the gracious drive and across the magnificent green lawns towards the Residency and thought to himself. 'Well mother dear, this is rather better than egg and tomato sandwiches with the Vicar.'

Sinclair soon settled into his office and found the work schedule outlined by his immediate superior Ted Bradshaw surprisingly straightforward and relaxed. He even had a ceiling fan for heaven's sake, albeit very much smaller than the ones in the Secretariat.

Twelve-noon found Sinclair back at the Hostel eating lunch and lying by the pool until the afternoon work session resumed at one thirty. He was astonished to find that the day's work really did finish at three thirty in the afternoon. Practically the middle of the day he thought. In fact, the work sessions seemed to be isolated patches in between food and fun.

Before he left the Hostel for the afternoon session he met up with several other Hostel residents. Four he liked immediately, Jacko, Norton, Sandy and Philip, and somehow, during the course of a fairly quick conversation, he had agreed to play squash at the Gymkhana Club later that evening and play tennis in Blantyre on Saturday.

Ted Bradshaw had invited him to dinner that evening and after he had showered and dressed in civvies, Sinclair relaxed on the deserted hostel veranda enjoying an ice-cold beer. Ted would be picking him up soon but he was quite glad of the quiet solitude in order to ponder on the way his new life was opening up.

Quite by chance, he caught sight of himself in an old mirror covered with fly droppings and gave a laugh and thought to himself, 'This all seems too good to be true, but there again, who cares, as long as it never changes.' He heard the promised car horn and hurried out to join Ted. But little did Sinclair know that the threat of change was already on the horizon.

CHAPTER EIGHT
PUTTING DOWN ROOTS

After a couple of weeks, Sinclair settled down to the routine of life at the hostel, congenial work in the office and evening fun at the Club. He met up briefly with his old school friend Lance Pearson who unfortunately was on immediate transfer to the Department of Information in Lilongwe.

"Almost as if they want to keep St. Aiden's Old Boys apart Sinclair! Never mind it will be somewhere for you to visit. We have a guesthouse right on the Lakeshore and there's a boat. Catch up on old times and have a few pots together hey!" Lance's voice faded away as the Land Rover drove off down towards Liwonde Ferry. "Try and make it next month if you can." Sinclair waved farewell. Such a pity Lance was going off immediately to Lilongwe but the prospect of a weekend at the Lake was promising. 'I want to see as much as possible of this incredible country,' he said to himself.

Over the next few days Sinclair explored Zomba and got to know fellow Civil Servants in the various Ministries and Departments dotted around the Capital. "Must be the smallest Capital in the world," he commented to Ted Bradshaw as they stood on the road above the old Tung Estate and looked over towards the shallow lake spread across the Palombe Plains. The bright sun lit up the dugout canoes used by the locals to catch fish, their daily relish. In the far

LAKE CHILWA:
Successful fishing is the result of the development of many age-old skills, which have been handed down from generation to generation. These include the art of traditional boat building together with the manufacture and repair of nets and fishing tackle. These villagers live on the shores of Lake Chilwa, a large, shallow stretch of natural water that spreads across the Palombe Plains close to Zomba.

distance on the Portuguese East Africa border, the Mulanje mountains looked almost mystical, swathed as they were in early morning mists and smoke from a thousand village fires. It was such an awe-inspiring, massive canvas that the two men fell silent, unwilling to break the magic of the moment.

Ted thought back on Sinclair's comment on Zomba. "Yes, you are right Sinclair whilst H.E. and the Secretariat remain here, Civil Service roots run deep so Zomba is top of the pile for now. Blantyre is the commercial capital of the country of course but who knows what will happen if and when Independence is granted to Nyasaland. Big changes are sweeping through Africa these days." Ted kicked a rather large stone in his path. "Ouch! You see, even talking about it makes me angry." "I can understand Ted, you all work so hard even if it is working in paradise!" They both laughed but Sinclair added, "I must admit I have been hearing a few rather disturbing things at the office. But surely Independence is still a long way off?"

"Who knows Sinclair? It seems that as soon as these African countries demand Independence, Britain pulls down the Union Jack fairly quickly. I understand there's a chance it might take place in under ten years. Already, two powerful black politicians, Henry Chipembere and Kanyama Chiume, who established the Nyasaland African Congress, have invited a Doctor Hastings Banda to return from the UK, where he has been practicing medicine. They want him to come back and take over the country."

"Shame that things have to change but that's progress for you. Mind you a lot of British blood, sweat and tears have gone into this country. Many dedicated and unsung men and women died here too. Actually my Great Uncle is buried here in Zomba, he was Postmaster General in the 1920s. Dear old Archie had the most magnificent tenor voice. Jolly popular at parties and concerts and always ready with jokes and stories too. A great asset to the community was Archie. Sad though. He died of blackwater fever, a fatal illness in those days."

Ted gestured with a wide sweep of his arm. "See this old Tung estate. Years ago, we produced some of the finest vegetable oil in the world on this hill. It was used to lubricate very delicate and specialised equipment and machinery. All went by the board when the oil companies started to produce fancy chemical oils. The price of progress I suppose!"

"But I can tell you, Sinclair, the estate personnel led a bloody wonderful life. I'll take you to see one of the retired Managers one day, Godwin Weatherspoon, God for short. He's a talkative old chap and still lives in one of the old estate houses. Gone bush of course and married a local called Beauty and they have five kids, but still a hell of a nice guy. He's an interesting old bugger. A few drinks and you really learn a lot about Zomba in the 1920s."

Ted waved towards a large old house tucked away in some enormous trees. "His house is a bit dilapidated now but he still employs his original staff who all come from the Fort Johnston area which was on the Arab slave trade route. Quite a colourful and dignified lot really, they all wear long white robes called kanzas, topped with a red fez. God insists that everything is carried to him on a silver tray, even his toothbrush. Actually I once saw Glorybe his cook carrying a full silver tea set and scones up the hill to the hospital when old God was being treated for a bout of malaria. He never trusted anyone else's tea, teapot or cup for that matter. He's from another era our God."

Sinclair was lost for words. It was all a bit mind-boggling really. He could not decide whether they were all a bit touched by the sun or just eccentric.

They continued to gaze across the plain, which seemed to undulate in the heat of the sun. It was almost hypnotic, in fact. Ted broke the silence. "See that small island over there?" He pointed to a rocky isle in the middle of the nearest lake. "They did a geological survey there recently and found that one side of the island is radio-active. The strange thing is that a small community live on the island and they don't seem to be affected in any way, no trouble in breeding, and no deformities whatsoever. The people are a fine looking lot really. But the situation has set the scientists in a buzz."

Somehow the two men found it difficult to break away from the scene. Sinclair pondered. How little impact man has made on nature in this country, miles of untouched bush in all directions. Ah well, there lies a challenge perhaps.

"Come on Sinclair, let's go to the Club and have a pint before lunch." Ted led the way down to his old Landie. "I'll take you via the hospital. I have to collect some malaria pills and it's a nice view. Hope you have some pills. Don't forget to take them every day otherwise you'll get into trouble if you get an attack of the old shivers. Black mark on your file you know." Sinclair looked at Ted and remembered the warnings given by HH in London. "I've got the pills Ted, but someone said that they ruin your eyes, make you deaf and do something to your love-life." Ted roared with laughter. "I don't know about your eye-sight or your love-life but better deaf than dead. Take your pills there's a good chap."

Each time Sinclair went to the Club he felt a sense of déjà vu. The gracious old lounge with its well-used comfortable furniture and quiet library graced by cabinets of sports trophies somehow reminded him of his old boarding school in Surrey. "Must have a good look through some of those old books one day," he said to Ted. "Can't waste good drinking time old lad," grinned Ted as he swept Sinclair through the ancient swing doors to the long bar, already filled with lunchtime members. The long open veranda was edged with sunshine, which lit up the rather moth-eaten game trophies and mildewed photographs of past Club chairmen.

"Come on Sinclair, hurry up man," shouted Jacko and as Sinclair turned towards the smiling faces and outstretched hands he almost felt tears coming into his eyes. Ted caught sight of his face and said quickly. "All a bit over-whelming eh Sinclair, never mind you'll soon be an old hand, new recruits arriving Monday." Ted and Sinclair were drawn into the crowd around the bar. The jokes and laughter resounded to the regular beat of "cheers."

Jacko whispered wickedly in Sinclair's ear. "Think this is heaven? We have a few other delights tucked up our sleeves. What say boys?" Philip, Sandy and Norton nodded vigorously. Jacko gave an evil wink, "This is only lunchtime old lad. Wait for the sun to go down to-night."

Sinclair roared with laughter. Even though he knew that the evening would probably end up at the bar again, maybe one or two of the stenographers will come into the Club for a drink and a laugh. Perhaps one of the new girls arriving tomorrow will be the girl of his dreams. That's how it was with Jacko's plans. Always a maybe, but who knows what tonight or tomorrow might bring. Yes, Jacko, his new friend, somehow brought an element of excitement to the dullest day. What a fantastic guy.

Sinclair raised his glass, "Cheers to a great bunch of people." To his surprise no one answered. In fact some drinkers were looking at him with expressions ranging from horror to disapproval. Even Jacko seemed to have turned his back on him.

"Steady on old lad, don't go overboard with the compliments." Ted drew him aside. "You see they've welcomed you, but they don't know you properly yet and so any sort of lavish talk at the bar is just not on. New recruits just don't call the tune. Let's slip away and have some lunch." Nothing more was said. Sinclair knew that he had broken some unspoken unwritten rules. 'First lesson learnt,' he thought to himself. Ted gave him a friendly punch on the arm. "You're a very nice young fellow, but take it slowly, slowly, pays in the end! Now what shall we have, curry or fish and chips?"

CHAPTER NINE
SINCLAIR GOES BUSH

Sinclair set his clock for a wake-up call at 4 a.m. His packet of sandwiches and thermos flask were ready and waiting and he was really looking forward to his first trip into the bush working at grassroots level. A first field day experience in fact. There was quite a gang of them going really. Two vehicle loads plus a Ministry of Information mobile unit and plenty of provisions, as they were to stay over-night at a rest-house way down near St. Joseph's Catholic Mission. A very hot area, apparently almost below sea level. Ted said it was a pretty basic rest house, no electricity, but with a wood stove for cooking, mosquito nets and a few beers, it was bearable. Dawn found them slithering down the unbelievably steep, narrow and winding Chikwawa escarpment road. Every so often someone had to hop out and remove small landslides of rocks and trees.

"Why in hell are we going down here in the rainy season?" shouted Anthony Hailsham, a visiting agricultural economist from Britain, as he rubbed a bruised ankle. "Because," said Ted Bradshaw patiently, "we have a situation on our hands. There are about twenty thousand people living in the Valley and their only income is from growing cotton. We know that's about a hundred pounds a year per family, but apart from paying extremely high prices for food from the local Indian stores; we know that they bury the rest in a tin under the family fireplace, which is a fairly fatal thing to do. Not only do the termites get into the tins, sometimes the tin collapses and the money is burnt and there's also a huge increase in community thieving. Sad really. It never happened in the past."

"Well anyway the Ministry of Posts wants to come in and set up a

THE CHIKWAWA VALLEY ROAD:

A typical low-level bridge that was a high risk for travellers in the rainy season. A flash flood high up in the mountain could, almost without warning, wash down a huge wall of trees and boulders sweeping vehicles, and people off the bridge and carrying them many miles downstream.

Post Office Savings Bank so they asked us to go in first and explain the system. Apparently research has shown that the rural people generally believe advice given by the Department of Agriculture. How's that lads?" A brief cheer broke out which died away as they turned the final corner and saw the valley floor. For as far as the eye could see hundreds of small streams racing across the terrain, which looked rather like a very old dried-out cheese. Some eroded gullies had deepened into ravines and had already filled up with rainwater. It looked like a driver's worst nightmare.

The group sat down and opened the flasks of coffee and tea. A decision had to be made, to go on or turn back. But as Ted pointed out, communities had gathered together from all over the valley and were waiting for them. The Department's good standing with them would be lost if they didn't turn up. Also they had to drop off the mail and rations for Father O'Connor at St Joseph's Mission. "Poor old chap has no vehicle and usually walks fifteen miles to Zomba to buy groceries and get his mail AND he's got a gammy leg. Metal plate on his shin, which has gone septic. Apparently he was a paratrooper during the war and during a jump over France, he was shot in the leg and never treated properly in the prisoner-of-war camp." Ted said.

"Never could understand these missionaries, devoting their lives to teaching the locals the three R's and the Bible." Percy Jones-Bayter snorted. "Well," said Ted mildly, "It seems to me that we Civil Servants are sort of missionaries. We do preach the gospel of wise rule and land conservation you know and we give our blessings in the form of Master Farmer badges and the odd gong," They all laughed and got back into the vehicles. It was going to be a rough ride.

After an hour or so of heavy going they drove out of a magnificent indigenous forest onto a wide green plateau over which a large attractive village sprawled. The fierce sun was already steaming the recent rainstorm out of the red soil as Ted shouted over the rattle and bangs coming from the old Land Rover. "We are coming to the first village, actually it's classified as the most remote and backward village in the whole of Nyasaland. Personally I think it is one of the most unspoilt and well cared-for communities in the country but we could have problems with this lot,"

Ted was right because the village of Mutenga was under the iron rule of Headman Issak Dondo and he was considered to be the biggest stumbling block in the path of agricultural progress. One of his greatest anti-success weapons at a Field Day was to stand up and say 'The spirits have told the people of Mutenga to follow the old ways'. "Nothing gets to them quite like the family spirits," Ted said sorrowfully. "We might as well pack up and go home if he brings up that chestnut." However the Headman kept quiet because this Field Day was about money, and there was definitely an air of interest floating above the six or seven hundred people sitting patiently in what Sinclair could only describe as 'the village square', a large area of dust swept clean of every stick and stone. An assortment of old chairs and stools had been placed in the shade of a large tree for the visiting officials.

After a great many, seemingly meaningless changes of position, within the ranks of the villagers, they all came forward, one by one, to shake hands with the visitors. It took a long time. The drums set up a rhythmic beat and the entire village commenced a lusty and very dusty dance. The rising red dust stuck to the heavy perspiration on the visitors' bodies and soon white skins took on a red-Indian glow. 'Damn uncomfortable,' thought Sinclair but he took a quick photograph of his colleagues. 'Mother will never believe this.'

The villagers, both men and women, were very well built and their skin was very black. "It's living down here in a regular temperature of over 140 degrees," Ted explained. The entire community wore the minimum of clothing, even the women, whose large and shining breasts leapt and danced in the sun.

"People would pay thousands overseas for this sort of entertainment," Percy Jones-Bayter whispered wickedly. But soon the meeting got under way and although there was little reaction to the plan by the villagers, Ted was confident that progress had been made. "Silence usually means that at least they will think about it but it will be a long haul I am sure. I once lectured a village for seven consecutive years on the value of building a bridge over a seasonal river. They listened courteously, never commented and they certainly took no action. In fact I was just about to give up when they finally agreed to give our ideas a try. Said they had to talk it all over first. I've learnt that you can't rush things in Africa."

As they drank a quick beer before going on to the next village, Sinclair saw a fine-looking old man sitting under a tree. His face looked as if it had been carved out of soapstone. Sinclair went up to him and asked if he could take a photograph of him. To his surprise the man spoke good English.

"Why do you come here to change our ways young Master? We are very content. I worked long and hard in the mines of South Africa all my life and I came back home with much money to buy three wives and many goats. I am a rich man but my money is not stored in a bank or in the ground, it is all around me." He indicated the wide range of children sitting near him. "Wives and children are the finest riches of Africa. Land and water and the food we grow, these we value more than money. Why must all things change?"

They looked at each other and suddenly Sinclair felt uncomfortable. 'Were they interfering unfairly in the lives of the community?' The old man continued, "And another thing young Master, recently the African politicians sent down a bus and we were forced to go up to Limbe to hear some madman shouting and screaming about freedom and fighting for our rights. Fighting for rights? What are rights? We do exactly what we want here. But eeee, that journey was terrible."

There was a moment's silence before he continued. "You see young Master now that I am old, all I want to do is sit under this thorn tree and smoke my pipe and remember my life, all that was good, all that was bad. I want to enjoy each day well. Is that too much to ask?" Sinclair didn't know what to say. Much of his immediate sympathy was with the old man but he felt he had to justify his visit. Surely development and change must be good he thought but when he looked around the clean village and saw the healthy, happy looking villagers a doubt crept into his mind. 'Are we doing all this for the right reasons, or are we just trying to impose a British way of life on our colonies!'

His thoughts were disturbed by a loud shout "Come on Sinclair, you don't want to miss the last bus home." He gave a laugh and hurried to join his companions. There must be a good reason for change. Just look at the calibre of these Civil Servants. First class chaps, dedicated and jolly good friends too. He shook off the doubt and jumped into the back of the Landie.

Onwards they went toiling from one village to another. "I guess we'll be down here for a week at least," said Anthony with a groan. "Absolute rubbish," replied Ted. "We must be back in Zomba by tomorrow evening, it's my daughter's birthday. Anyway we only have food for two days, so that's that."

The day seemed endless, but towards four o'clock they found themselves by the side of a large river with a small backwater of reasonably clear water.

"Water's not too brown today so it's time for a wash and brush up lads," announced Percy and soon all the men had stripped off, whilst Percy set up a small card table covered with a white cloth and cups and saucers. Sinclair was astounded, 'what about bilharzia,' he thought but as nobody else seemed particularly worried he jumped into the water. The quick wash certainly made him feel a great deal more comfortable and once he had put on a clean shirt he felt ready for anything, even travel onto the next village seemed possible.

"Tea, gentlemen?" Percy inquired with a flask poised at the ready. "I have some rather nice digestive biscuits too." Sinclair looked around the group. Nobody seemed to be in the least surprised at the development of a suburban tea party in the middle of nowhere.

"Where's the silver tea-pot Percy?" He asked with a note of laughter in his voice but Percy played it back with a perfectly straight face. "My pot can only serve six people, not eight, so sorry old chap, today we'll have to make do with the flasks."

'Good heavens,' thought Sinclair, 'this is like something out of a 1920 village play,' However as he sat watching the men downing their tea along with idle chatter in the middle of raw bush he realised that this simple ritual was more than just a leftover from a British way of life. It was an anchor of discipline. It was a contact with 'back home'. It was the sort of routine action that made British colonial civil servants famous throughout the world.

"Cheers, here's to us," Sinclair raised his cup in acknowledgement to his colleagues. "Good gracious, it's too early for cheers, Sinclair." Percy wagged a finger at the Junior Officer. "Don't buck the system my boy, we'll stop and toast Her Majesty the Queen at six o'clock, after which you can toast anything you like."

Later as they stood together under a huge thorn tree brightly lit by a rising moon Sinclair felt close to tears as Percy, stood to attention, raised his glass and said "Gentlemen, Her Majesty the Queen." The following chorus of voices hid Sinclair's rather weak response. Suddenly he felt very homesick indeed.

Whether it was just coincidental or whether Ted understood the situation, he slapped Sinclair round the shoulders "Good to have you aboard my boy." Ted never quite forgot his war years on a minesweeper. "Hope the first day was not too traumatic for you." He turned to the rest of the group. "Let's get on over to the Rest House, have supper and a bit of a sing-song, what say?"

Later that evening as the Rest House rang to a surprisingly harmonious rendering of "Land of Hope and Glory", followed by a rowdy version of "Sweet Violets" by Percy. After the laughter died down and some of the men had wandered off to bed, Sinclair walked out onto the veranda and gazed on the wide expanse of bush in front of the building.

The sharp spiky shapes of the thorn trees were heightened by the full moon. Unknown and exotic perfumes drifted in on the tail of an evening breeze. There was a magical quality to the moment. Quite suddenly, and without warning, a leopard strode majestically across the open ground in front of the Rest House. It turned and looked at Sinclair full in the face, tail lashing the ground with yellow eyes blazing. 'The final cherry on top of the cake,' thought Sinclair as he went back to share a last drink with his friends. 'I'm a very lucky chap indeed'.

CHAPTER TEN
LOOKING FOR FEMALE COMPANY

Jacko burst into the communal sitting room at the Government Hostel. His four friends and fellow Civil Servants were already on their fourth beer after a hot day's work in Mid-October.

"Cheer up lads, some good news," Jacko beamed as he caught the beer bottle flung expertly into his outstretched hand. His wild head of curly red hair, which would never conform to Civil Service regulations, seemed to reflect his excitement. "Females on the way, and I think we should go out to Chileka Airport, look over the new talent and, according to our scoring, give them a rousing welcome."

A clamour of excited questions interrupted further details until Jacko held up his hands, "Hold on lads, my secret informer whispered only a few details." His friends exchanged knowing looks. They were all well aware that Jacko was looking after the Administrative Officer's wife Kate, in more ways than one. Behind his back they affectionately called him 'Keyhole Jack'!

Jacko consulted his scrap of paper. "Five nurses and four stenographers arriving, wait for it.... tomorrow, Sunday! We've got plenty of time to get ready and arrange a personalised welcome. Don't forget, it's a secret score of one to ten and, by the way lads, I get first choice."

Cheers and laughter filled the room but gradually the young men slipped away to check on best shirt, clean socks and how much was left of last Christmas's after-shave. The next day saw them all polished and shining and standing in a row at the airport. All eyes were on the aircraft as the door swung open. The wait seemed endless. Firstly and astonishingly, two nuns stepped out onto the tarmac and blessed themselves. "No score and that's two nurses off the list," muttered Norton.

Behind them came a small, plump girl with thick glasses. As she smiled up at them they saw with horror the huge gap between her front teeth. "Must smoke a pipe! What about 3 points? She has got beautiful blue eyes you know?" Sinclair giggled into his freshly starched handkerchief. Miss 3 points was followed by a very tall and freckled 5 points redhead and a sturdy girl with very pink cheeks and well-developed calves.

"Bet she's one of those Irish dancers, leaping all over the place and wriggling her ankles. Definitely only a 5," muttered Philip. There was an air of depression, which Jacko was determined to break. "Well lads, we'll need nursing through our malaria and hangovers so with this little gaggle of feminine charm, we are looking at friendship of the purest kind. Continue to keep your eyes open and let's make do and mend lads," boomed Jacko. "Still four stenographers to come."

As three of the four remaining females stepped off the plane, the welcoming party saw that they were definitely not in the first flush of youth. All wore identical, very sensible, lightweight coats and skirts. "A fine display of Army and Navy Store clothing," Jacko observed. But he also noticed that one had a twinkle in her eye and a splendid bust-line. She looked up and waved to the lads. Might be a bit of hope there he thought, as he turned to his companions.

"Abandon hope all ye who got up at 6am to get here today, let's go lads and drown our sorrows at Limbe Club." They were just turning away when there was a gasp from Sandy. "Look lads." They gazed in wonder as a Venus-shaped blond undulated across the tarmac. "Can't be! Could it be? don't forget lads I have first choice." Jacko vaulted the barrier and rushed to carry a shining vanity case. Gloria Campbell smiled, embracing them all with her presence. She was used to causing a stir but hadn't expected it quite so early in the morning in Africa.

To a man they were smitten and the other eight women melted into the background. Gold had been struck. The journey had been worth it after all.

The journey back to Zomba saw four frustrated men crammed into the overheated back of a very ancient Land Rover, with Jacko driving and Gloria beside him, both blissfully unaware of the misery under the canopy. A small bus followed with the other passengers and all Gloria's luggage.

During the following months, Gloria managed to share her company quite successfully with all of the five young men, but only in a group. It seemed she had no inclination to go out with only one of them at a time. In fact, company was all she did share, and they were all racking their brains as to how to bring her down from the pedestal and into one of the five waiting pairs of welcoming arms and possibly individual beds.

"Blow it all, Gloria, we've pooled all our funds to give you a very special evening, how can you let us down again," grumbled Jacko one evening when once more she had cancelled a plan to go over to Blantyre for dinner and the flicks because of pressure of office work. "My darlings, the boss is frightfully busy these days with all these pre-Independence discussions, I just can't say no to him," She giggled and wound a loose golden curl round her finger as she waved goodbye to the five very-fed-up young men.

The silent group watched her fascinating departure as she negotiated the brick-lined path on six-inch heels. “There’s more to this than meets the eye, me boyos, let’s do a spot of follow-up,” growled Jacko. Later in the evening, the gang crept up to the nearby Secretariat and noticed Gloria’s modest Mini parked next to the big white Mercedes. Worming their way around the building they reached the windows of the new Board Room. All the lights were on.

“Funny! Why would they be working in there,” said Jacko thoughtfully. “Perhaps because the building is raised on concrete stilts to ward off termites and intruders,” said Philip with a quiet giggle. ‘Never a truer word spoken in jest perhaps,’ Jacko thought.

“Come over here Sandy, you’re the lightest, we’ll give you a bunk up, no need for us all to look.” Norton put his smaller friend on his massive shoulders and slowly raised him up. There was a long silence. “What’s the problem Sandy, tell us what’s going on,” said Jacko impatiently. “Good gracious,” whispered Sandy. “I say, quick put me down and let’s get out of here.” Sandy looked quite pale as they half dragged him at top speed back to the Hostel where they gave him a stiff drink. “You’ll never believe it lads,” croaked Sandy. “There they were both starkers and they were, you know whatwhating, on that new Board Room table.” A strange silence fell on the group as each listener registered the news.

“So that’s why he wanted a thick felt lining under the leather covering,” said Jacko thoughtfully to himself. “Now we have to make a bit of hay out of this sunshine, old lads. You know what I mean, a whisper or two. 'She’s a bit of all right eh Sir' when he’s three sheets to the wind at the next cocktail party. What say chaps? Might help us climb up the fragile promotion ladder.” Jacko smiled.

There was deep silence as they all took a deep swallow of the new local gin Jacko had just purchased from Kandodo Store. Faces turned blue and purple and a cacophony of spluttered coughing filled the air. “What the hell are you doing to us Jacko, that’s seared the lining off my stomach,” whispered Philip weakly. “Keep saying to yourself it only costs five bob a bottle, old dear. You’d be surprised how it helps the medicine go down,” said Jacko cheerfully.

The young men leaned back and closed their eyes and settled back to enjoy a variety of mental pictures of what Sandy saw. “You know lads, Gloria isn’t that marvellous starkers.” Sandy muttered. “Matter of fact she has warts on her back and I could have sworn she saw me and winked.”

“Look Gloria’s a write-off, no ways can we muscle in on forbidden territory. Let’s consider the rest, how about those nurses?” Jacko took out a list. “All three Irish and Catholic. Short fat Irish one is Eileen O’ Sullivan, tall thin job is Shael O’Shea and the sturdy one in the middle is Bernadette Ryan. Let’s make a three-pronged attack.”

But no matter how many different ways the boys tried to contact the three girls they were either on duty; sleeping after night duty; mysteriously unavailable or their communal house was filled with Irish priests and brothers from the nearby Mission.

The boys agreed to try different times of the day and so one morning Norton knocked on the front door, bunch of wild flowers in hand, only to be faced by an enraged nurse dressed in a flowery nightie and with rag curlers in her hair. “I couldn’t understand a word she was saying old dears, especially with all the spit shooting out at me from between the two front teeth. Gathered she had just come off night duty and was EXHAUSTED and she would never consider going out with a dirty Britisher. She went on at length about Prison ships and four million Irishmen being used as cannon fodder by Butcher Haig at the Battle of the Somme. In the end I was backing down the path and she was advancing shaking her fist. Thank God there was no shillelagh to hand. Wow, what a terrible experience.”

Sinclair leaned back on the veranda chair and closed his eyes. He really wasn't keen to get involved with a girl at this stage of his life. Sleepily he pondered over Norton's tale of woe. Never did go along entirely with the jolly smiling Irish leprechaun image myself. Always thought they were a bit short tempered and heaven knows how they remember every detail of the 'Trouble'. 'No I think I'll go for a nice predictable English girl,' and with that promise, he fell asleep.

CHAPTER ELEVEN
AFTERNOON TEA AT THE MISSION

Philip burst into the sitting room and flung himself into a chair. "Spicy news boys, my laundry boy, Jairos has a girl friend at Kalunga Mission and he said the Mission cook, One-Finger, told him that the priests talk in a strange language when the hospital nurses come to visit." The junior officers, mildly interested, looked up from their game of Monopoly. Philip saw they were interested and went on. "Well apparently they then have a few drinks and start singing wild songs all about 'bayonets glistening in the sun' and 'blood flowing in the streets.' Then before they leave all the nurses kneel down with the priests and seem to chant spells using magic words. They keep looking at some little bead necklaces too. One-Finger thinks that they are talking to bad spirits and says no one should work at the Mission."

"Good story Phil, but I've got some real spicy details for you lads," Jacko said cheerfully. "It was too wet for golf and so I decided to pop into the Club to have a glass and chat. There were quite a few people at the bar but as I went in, I saw Bernadette coming out of the library, so I invited her for a drink and to my amazement she accepted. Sadly, I had to order two lemonades but that seemed to soften her nicely and just when I thought a spot of how's-your-father at the back of the squash court might be possible, suddenly all hell broke loose as old Stuart Charlton-Potts galloped across the cricket pitch on his horse Rosy Posy. Thought it was the Queen's birthday you see and came to the Club to toast Her Majesty's health. Couldn't be persuaded it was not the right date. Rode right up the veranda steps and demanded a g and t for himself and the horse. The horse pinched all the peanuts too. Of course Rosy dropped a large amount of pooh and then old Potty fell out of the saddle and into you know what. Finally he thought he was back in India and started to lay about with his crop. Knocked poor old Chalky White off his stool and Chalky lost his false teeth in the melee, so I backed off. Got a bit splattered though, very nasty."

There was silence as the group pondered upon Jacko's experience. "Good heavens Jacko, what a story but come to think of it, you do pong a bit, but carry on with the Bernadette story," said Sinclair impatiently. Jacko settled down into a more comfortable chair.

"Well she said she had to be going and something made me follow her and her old Morris as it toiled all the way up through the mountain mists to the Mission. Thought to myself, she's probably going to confession before Mass tomorrow," Jacko held up a restraining hand. "Yes lads, you may murmur in disbelief but I do know about these things. Anyway, I crept up to a window in that big old dining room thinking I might hear a thing or two but it seemed to be a rather sedate tea party. All the priests and brothers gave her a great welcome after she presented them with a big fruitcake sent by her Irish mammy. You know fierce Irish hugs and all that."

"Then the Mission cookie came in with the tea tray. But, and wait for it boys, when the tea was poured out it looked like water. Holy water I thought to myself, until the party started to get riotous and then I heard Father Pat say, 'Brendan, me brother, ye've excelled yourself this month. This is without doubt the finest poteen ever brewed in this country. It's even better than me Da's brew in West Cork.'

The boys rolled on the floor weak with laughter. "Can you believe it", shouted Sandy "and there's that Father Pat refusing a beer last week, said he'd signed the pledge when he was fifteen years old and never a drop of the hard stuff touched his lips since then."

"And neither has it," said Jacko, "Straight down the throat it goes. But let me get on with the story," Soon Father Michael got out his fiddle and Bernadette put on her dancing shoes and there they all were leaping and prancing and giving wild Irish shouts as a full-blown ceilidh went into top gear. "I was mesmerised boys, simply glued to the spot, and especially by Bernie's knickers all be-dressed with little red hearts but then something happened." Jacko had their full attention.

"I heard another vehicle grinding up the road. Luckily I had hidden my motorbike behind that smelly outside chimbuzi. The wild party-makers heard the approaching car too. Evidently it was a familiar engine. Anyway by the time the Bishop had got out of the car and I had turned back to the fascinating party scene, a miraculous change had taken place. There they all were down on their knees praying, Bernie too, with Ignatius the cook coming in through the door with a real pot of tea and a plate of scones."

Bishop Mahoney beamed as he took in the full canvas. 'My dear Father Pat, you seem to be sweating, not malaria I hope.' 'Sure Glory be to God, My Lord, 'tis the jogging. Up and down the mountain I go twice a day, just as I did on Mt. Kid in Ballydehob, keeping the devil at bay,' gasped Father Pat, who by now could see two Bishops.

'Well done, my son, well done,' the Bishop reached for the milk jug. 'I say there seems to be just water in this jug.' Before he could say another word, the jug was whisked out of his hands and given to Ignatius 'Now what the devil are you doing Ignatius giving the poor Bishop water to put in his tea, off with ye and get some milk from the goat outside,'

Father Pat turned to the Bishop and told him, 'I advised Ignatius not to take a Jesuit name when he was baptised. I said it would turn his brain. But since we have seven staff named Francis and five of them called Patrick, he decided as chief cook he should be different. Glory be to God, the cheek of the man.'

Jacko continued. "Before I left me boyos, sadly I heard the Bishop talking to Bernadette about entering and I gather she is becoming a Poor Clare. So we can strike her name off the list." Jacko looked inquiringly round as the boys nodded in agreement. "Interesting though about the Mission activities. We must try and time our visits right next time. What about getting them a liquor licence Sandy? Could you swing it?" Sandy looked thoughtful. He was rather strait-laced over his office work. "I'll give it some thought Jacko," he said doubtfully.

There was a long pause while the boys pondered upon the Mission story. Sinclair, in some curious way, felt let down. He had written to his mother telling her about the work of the Mission and how they were running a school and clinic for the locals. He actually thought they were all quite saintly people. But then maybe they were. Perhaps they just had to have some kind of safety valve to keep them from going bushed or potty. Yes, that's right, they are only human, must have a bit of fun. He felt better.

Jacko called the meeting to order. "Back to business lads, let's consider the balance of females left. How about throwing a party, a fancy dress party, better still a candlelit fancy dress party. It will give them a chance to hide their discrepancies. It's called making a silk purse out of a sow's ear." He roared with laughter and they all joined in. A party would be just the thing, just wonderful. Their laughter spread through the Hostel and woke Andy from his afternoon nap.

"Now what are they up to," he growled to Maggie his wife. "Mischief

I'll be bound". "But they're a grand bunch, I'll miss them if they move out," Maggie replied and smiling went back to sleep.

Strangely enough the very next day, Jacko rushed in at lunchtime with some exciting news. "I say chaps I've just been told about some new digs. About time we left the Hostel. Apparently there's a big old house going vacant next month. It's further up the hill and near the Club. The Housing Officer suggests we all move in together and run a sort of Mess. Any of you game? If you agree we can move in at the end of the month!"

Cheers broke out on all sides. "Not that we haven't enjoyed our time at the Hostel, Andy old dear," Norton said, when later they went to tell the Hostel warden their news. "Time we moved on you see, put up a few pictures, organise our own food and get a bit domesticated. Will miss you and Maggie very much, but its time we grew up and did our own things."

Later that week, Sinclair wrote to his mother. *'Mum you cannot believe our new quarters. Rooms ramble in all directions and the view from the veranda looking towards the Mulanje Mountains is so beautiful. The garden is filled with frangipani and bougainvillea and there's a veggie garden well protected from the small buck that sneak down from the mountain and forage for fresh green food. We share expenses and already we've had two parties. It's really great Mother dear, you must come out and have a good long rest here one day.'*

CHAPTER TWELVE
THE FANCY DRESS PARTY

The veranda of the new house was lit by candles stuck rather haphazardly in a variety of bottles, silent tribute to past parties, but as Jacko looked round critically he remarked "Well boys, the scenery is just right, the lighting is low to the point of dangerous, all we need now are the actors and actresses and here they come."

They all watched eagerly as a long line of car-lights snaked up the hill towards the house. "Into action lads and remember it's every man for himself tonight." Jacko adjusted his Robin Hood bow and arrow into a less dangerous position and cast a critical eye over his friends. "I say guys why didn't you fellows get together, Two Clark Gables, one Charlie Chaplin and a Roy Rogers is a bit over the top."

The four men shuffled sheepishly trying to remove pieces of Hollywood identification. One wicked moustache went into a flower vase and the cigarette holder fell into a deadly punch, made up of dregs drained from a dozen old bottles of nameless spirits and ancient liqueurs. "I added a couple of bottles of local gin for good measure, guaranteed to break down the strongest resistance," whispered Jacko out of the corner of his mouth.

The single male guests came first and took up a position of advantage to view the arriving talent. Next came the married couples with the single women arriving last to make an entrance, and make an entrance indeed they did. A silence fell upon the gathering whilst an assessment was being made. 'Were these females going to be a threat', thought the wives. 'Were they going to be available', thought the men.

The Irish nurses had gone local and bought caftans and headgear, but the four stenographers, Iris, Gloria, Maud and Letitia undulated into the party in the most amazing range of belly-dancing outfits. "They must have hired them from the Props Room at the Club." said Sinclair, "Gloria looks great as usual but just look at Latitia, go for it girl!" Silence fell as one of the girls performed the most beautiful and complicated and very professional belly dance. "I wonder where her last post was, Aden perhaps." Sandy gasped, "Forget her face old dears, just look at that splendid and enormous bust."

One of the older men, standing at the bar, let out a long sigh. With a bullied wife and five children, three from two previous marriages, Freddie Bones was known as a "tits" man and he was now gazing at the 'crême de la crême'.

"Look at that beautiful body", he breathed, "I've got to get to know that gorgeous creature." As if drawn by an irresistible force 'Boooossoms' as she came to be known, looked up and automatically turned sideways. Freddie was lost from that moment. He moved to her side and they spent the rest of the evening dancing in a bemused fashion, joined in spirit, but certainly held apart by the enormous barrier of mutual attraction. Nothing and no one could get between them. Not even Jacko's hellfire curry.

"Where's poor old Mabel this evening?" Sinclair hissed fiercely. "The kids are down with malaria," whispered Norton. "But don't worry he does this sort of thing quite regularly, always goes back home. But God knows why she takes him back." But this time it was not the same.

Eventually at the end of the next school-term, Freddie took his long-suffering wife and five children over to Glasgow and managed to leave them there. "Problems with schooling here," he announced when he returned triumphantly. Sadly no one asked about Mabel. No one mentioned divorce. There was a deafening silence and Freddie's threatening stare held off any comment or enquiry. In fact the truth of the matter was nobody cared very much and some people were frankly looking forward to the next sequence of events. As Jacko remarked, "Nothing like a bit of sordid gossip to keep a dinner party going, especially when the wine's not that great."

After a few months of hot fire passion, Boooossoms and Freddie became engaged and soon after lavish wedding invitations were posted. Next a wedding present list was established at Lulats store. The scene was set and everyone waited in expectation for the curtain to rise. And rise it did on the most extraordinary Zomba wedding of all time, held in an upstairs chapel, in a rather dingy building, round the back of the Indian market.

Jacko, who was always invited to everything, reported that, as Boooossoms sailed down the aisle, resplendent in white satin and accompanied by eight bridesmaids of varying ages, dressed in some unbelievable rainbow material, the harmonium driven by Granny Longspear burst into "O Perfect Love." A myriad of chapel voices gave it stick. This was a marriage made in heaven and not one conventional ritual would be ignored. The wedding cake was a marvel of confectionery and even the little bride figure seemed to thrust out its bust-line as if to say, "This is how I did it." The reception speeches were filled with magnificent praise for Boooossoms and even if Freddie had supposedly been through the whole process at least three times before he managed to look suitably bashful in the right places.

Some years later, as Jacko was helping Sinclair pack up his modest library before leaving Malawi for the last time, he spied an old photograph album. "Good Lord", said Jacko "Remember old Freddie and Boooossoms." Look at this photograph I took at their wedding." They gazed fascinated by the vision in white and Freddie's gleaming eyes fastened on the massive curves.

"But you know old lad, when they went back to the UK he was arrested for bigamy. Seems he never bothered to get divorced from at least two of his previous wives. I gather Mabel went on the rampage and then took him back. Apparently he was secretly hankering for her steak and kidney pudding. Ah well there's nowt so funny as folk." Jacko leant back and closed his eyes. "No idea what happened to Boooossoms."

"What about the other stenogs?" Sinclair asked. "Well old dear, poor old Maudie went after Mick McNaulty and got preggers. Went down South to have the babe and put it up for adoption. Mick was furious. He had been waiting for a son and heir off his wife for years. Iris is shacked up with someone in the Outer Hebrides and Gloria was killed in a riding accident years ago."

"The nurses, well they are quite a different story. Quite a 'News of the World' story in fact." Jacko settled back with his beer. "You see one of the nuns abandoned the veil and married Brother Silas from one of the Missions up North. Then Father Pat, who always said that he was ordered to the Seminary to take the priesthood by his mother and six sisters, fell madly in love with Eileen O'Sullivan and off they went to Rome to get a dispensation. I believe they are living in Liverpool and have six kids. Funny how life turns out?"

The two men pondered on Jacko's words. Sinclair thought to him self, 'It's strange that even in the orderly society of the British Civil Service, things don't turn out as you expect.'

CHAPTER THIRTEEN
SINCLAIR VISITS THE GINNERY

The AE, Agricultural Officer, Framsham Potts called Sinclair into his office. "Feel up to carrying out a visit on your own Brown"? Fram raised his enormously bushy eyebrows and fixed Sinclair with a somewhat steely look.

"Perfectly confident Sir," Sinclair replied. "Where do I go, what do I do and when do I leave Sir?" But after Fram has explained the assignment Sinclair wasn't so sure. It sounded as if he had been passed a hot potato. Still a challenge was a challenge and he might as well get it over with as soon as possible.

Funny though, the AE said very emphatically, "Now don't bother to telephone ahead Sinclair, just sort of drop in by chance. OK? Off you go then." A couple of hours later Sinclair stopped his car and gazed thoughtfully at the ramshackle cotton ginnery in the middle of a wild area of bush. Nobody appeared to be around. He bent down to collect his briefcase from the floor of his car and straightened up to find a double-barrelled shotgun filling the car window. There behind it with furious eyes beading down the sights was MacTavish.

"Good morning," said Sinclair nervously offering a handshake. "Sinclair Brown from the Department of Agriculture. Just come for a routine safety check, Mr. MacTavish". "Get off me land," roared the ginnery owner. "I'll no have Goverrrrrment offishuls on me properrrty. You're all a lot of lily-livered pestulating parrrrasites. I'll no have ye here, now away with ye before I lose me temper." He gesticulated with his ancient weapon.

"Now look here Mr MacTavish, I understand how you feel, but quite honestly, I've only just started working for the Department and this first visit to you is a sort of special test. I am really more worried about what the AE and the Permanent Secretary will say if you make it difficult for me. I just have to carry out the Survey. There's the Annual Report you see," Sinclair swallowed hard and waited for the explosion and subsequent pain, but to his surprise after a moment's breathtaking pause, MacTavish put down the gun and offered a grimy hand through the window.

"You're an honest and polite young feller. Jock's me name. I've decided on the spur of the moment, as ye might say, to let ye in. However, I'll brook no criticism and mind no talking to me staff. Come this way." He led Sinclair into a battered old shed where, perched precariously on planks balanced on piles of old bricks, a score or so of workers were operating the rusty dilapidated machinery.

Steam gushed, power cables sloshed in pools of water and it appeared to Sinclair that the entire workforce was not concentrating on production, but on dodging the moving machinery and staying alive. During the long and horrifying tour around the complex MacTavish shouted constant and incomprehensible orders to the workforce who did not appear to hear or understand. Certainly there was absolutely no response or increase in the production line.

Afterwards sitting down with MacTavish in his box of an office and faced with a mug of tea that looked like Brown Windsor soup, Sinclair felt he must make some comment. He cleared his throat several times and tried to think of the right words to use. "Well Jock, very interesting, very busy, but do you find that you lose a number of staff per year through injury?"

The old man gazed back unflinchingly at him. "I hope young feller, that you are not forrming the same blasted opinnnnnion as all the other useless individuals from your office. One knock-kneed individual had the nerve to say that the whole factory should be closed down but he hadn't got the nerve to come and do just that after I ran him off me place, aye, and peppered his tyres with me gun. Now ye were asking about me staff getting hurt. Well I have me methods ye understand. I keeps a first aid box, iodine and sticky plaster and such trash but I don't keep a staff book. They comes and goes ye understand. However, ye might say I count them up at the beginning of the season and I count them up at the end and there's nay grreat discrerrpancy."

Sinclair downed the hot sweet tea and gazed thoughtfully at the battered old face, be-whiskered and grimy and yet somehow strangely lovable. However let's be practical, he thought, what can I say back at the office, even more ghastly what could he put in the report.

MacTavish's hand snaked under the desk and brought up a bottle of Johnnie Walker. "Ye'll have a dram young feller?" The thick, spiky eyebrows lowered. Sinclair knew it was a test. In fact it was a command more than a suggestion. "Bit early Sir. Sun's not over the yardarm yet." Sinclair murmured weakly. "Ouch ye Sassenach, my yardarm comes up as I eat my morning porridge, it is no wonder you English are such a lily-livered lot." MacTavish poured a very generous double tot into Sinclair's tea and there was nothing he could do but pick up the mug and down it.

After an hour and another generous splash into his mug, the Ginnery began to look like a Booneville factory to Sinclair and after two hours, MacTavish assumed the cloak and personality of Father Christmas. An incomprehensible Father Christmas because by now the golden liquid had reached the Scotsman's tongue and although Sinclair was vaguely aware of slushes and ucks pouring out of MacTavish's mouth not a word did he understand. However MacTavish did not want to be understood, he just wanted a captive listener and Sinclair found that an occasional lift of the teacup with a 'cheers' indicated his continuing interest.

As the sun started to go down over the nearby lake, Sinclair took his leave and after many a slap on the back and vows of undying friendship he managed to get into his vehicle and totter off down the dirt track.

On the rather perilous journey back along the dusty road he had a flash of genius. I know he thought happily, I'll tell them at the office that MacTavish was away in Limbe. It may only put off the evil day but it will solve the problems of this one. But as he drove into the driveway of his house, Samson came rushing out. "Telephone bwana, big chief." It was the Agricultural Officer. "Just had a surprise call from MacTavish, Sinclair, says he likes you. Only wants to deal with you in future and all that sort of thing. What happened? Anyway must go, look forward to your report with great interest."

He rang off and Sinclair sat down weakly. He closed his eyes and thought of his report which he had to put on the AE's desk tomorrow morning. Perhaps he could phrase it differently; 'staff records are taken at the beginning of the season and a further check is carried out at the end of the season and the slight difference in figures could be discounted as a labour fall-out.'

The next day he nervously presented the report to Fram who, without opening it, tossed the paper into a large box marked 'Safety Checks'. "Thanks my boy for a job well done. Can't imagine what happened between you and MacTavish but you've got him for the rest of your stint here. It will certainly look good on your report, 'Sinclair Brown has proved himself able to handle difficult customers' and all that."

Sinclair smiled gratefully. The thoughts of a New Year's Honour gong flashed through his mind. Must write to Mother dear tonight and tell her of my first successful assignment. Fram looked up from his desk. "You still here? It's alright, you can go off now Sinclair, see you at the Club for a pint tonight!"

"Right ho Sir, and thanks, see you later." Sinclair grinned and bounced out the door. 'Drinks with the boss tonight, I'm coming up the ladder Mother dear.'

That night Sinclair tottered into bed, having entertained the entire Club continuously from 4pm until midnight with the story of MacTavish and his Ginnery. He must have downed at least ten beers, all freebies from grateful listeners. 'If I keep this up I'll either end up an alcoholic or as a Permanent Secretary.' Just before he fell asleep he said to himself. 'One day though, I'll write a book about all this.'

In 1958 Doctor Hastings Banda returned to Nyasaland to head the fight for Independence as the chosen leader of the country.

CHAPTER FOURTEEN
SINCLAIR MEETS HIS MATE

"Oh Lord, yet another letter from mother asking me when I am going to come home and marry Emma." Sinclair groaned. "Who is Emma and why the lamentations old lad?" Jacko looked up from his latest Playboy. "Well, Emma lives next door and we grew up together and everyone wants us to marry but neither of us do. She's a nice kid but I know she would hate Africa. She has all the wrong colouring, blondish-redhead, freckles and pale skin. Hates spiders too. Wouldn't do at all." Sinclair cast his mind back to some of the little adventures he had shared with Emma, I rather miss the cuddles and kisses in the summerhouse, but where was the fire and the passion. No definitely Emma would not do.

It was Saturday morning and both Jacko and Sinclair felt lazy and relaxed. Golf was a lunch away with the chance of a party developing at the Club after a bracing shower and a piri-piri chicken supper. Prince, the house-servant, was dabbing ineffectively at some hornets' nests and spider-webs firmly housed in the sagging ceiling boards. The falling debris crunched under his bare feet. Bees droned, the coffee pot was nearly boiling and the beer was cooling in the fridge. It was a grand day.

Jacko was in the middle of telling Sinclair a hilarious story about Captain Harrington's eccentric mother, the Hon Hortense, as she was called. Apparently during her weekly bridge game in their lovely old thatched house some two miles outside of Zomba, her cook ran into the drawing room carrying a flaming chip pan and shouting 'Madam, Madam, the house is on fire'. Poor old Boatman must have been distraught but Hortense was very cross with him. I think she must have had a winning hand, anyway she was furious that the game was being interrupted and fixing the distraught cook with a fierce look, she roared, 'What the devil are you doing Cook, pick up the card tables and chairs and carry them carefully onto the lawn. We will continue playing there!' No thought given to Harrington's lovely house filled with rare antiques. Boatman ran all the way to Zomba to get help but the house was burnt to the ground. Can you imagine how poor old Ian felt coming back from manoeuvres in Muzuzu to find his house gone?

Suddenly the telephone rang, disturbing the laughter. "If it's the PS wanting me to do duty at Government House, tell him I've gone away for the day." Jacko bolted through the front door and onto his motorbike. Still laughing, Sinclair answered the phone, 'must be a wrong number he thought.'

"Hello, may I speak to Sinclair Brown." a charming voice spoke softly into Sinclair's ear. "Err, yes of course, it's me, I mean I am Sinclair Brown." Sinclair stuttered and swore inwardly. No one should upset the Saturday morning equilibrium.

"My name is Cynthia Lilford-Lewis and my mother Emmeline is a second cousin on your mother's side. Perhaps you've heard of her? Anyway, I've come to stay with my aunt Jo on their tea estate in Cholo and we were wondering if you could come over for lunch tomorrow." There was a long silence. Sinclair was speechless. Nobody had ever asked him anywhere outside of the Civil Service and he certainly had never heard of Mum's cousin Emmeline. He pondered a little and then thought 'she's made a mistake - but who cares.' Lost in the strangeness of the situation, he continued to hold the telephone to his ear but remained silent.

"Hello, hello, are you still there?" Cynthia raised her voice a few delicious decibels. "Yes, yes, I'm still here, just a bit bowled over. Of course I would like to come. What time? How do I get there?" Sinclair knew he was burbling but he'd been caught off balance. Wonder what she is like, he thought, lovely voice but I guess she is fair, fat and forty. Ah well, anything for a change of scenery.

Next morning, after a worrying search and the important and rather complicated route instructions found, Sinclair drove his old Vauxhall Polly through a pair of astonishingly imposing gates and into the most glorious garden he had ever seen. A wide dam fringed with flowering bushes and trees framed massive lawns broken only by masses of colourful flowerbeds. He could see a boat on the dam and someone fishing.

As Sinclair drove up to the portico, the front door was opened wide by a butler; dressed in what seemed to be Napoleonic costume. The vision gave a deep bow. "Welcome Sir, Madam and the young Mistress await you in the drawing room. The Master is fishing."

Madam? Mistress? Master? Sinclair felt that he had been transported back in time and lost in another era. However when he walked into the enormous and flower-filled room and gazed into Cynthia's smiling and lovely face he felt his heart miss a beat. 'Must be indigestion' he thought. But oddly enough he got the feeling that there was something special between them already. He could have sworn he heard heavenly music and looked around. "Piped Strauss music throughout the house," whispered Cynthia wickedly.

Lady Johanna Fostlewaite-Aird noticed the emotionally charged meeting and smiled gently to herself. Marriage may be made in heaven but the good Lord needs a bit of help here and there to make things happen. You owe me one cousin Emmeline.

Later in the day, after a seven-course lunch, which was served by waiters wearing white gloves, onto a table groaning with ancient silver and crystal, Cynthia took him on a tour of the house. "This is the bedroom wing. Each of the ten bedrooms is en suite and with a personal balcony, as they say in the brochure. This is the family chapel, note the Florentine decor. Good heavens I sound like a Cooks Travel Tour."

They both laughed as they climbed the tower. Sinclair caught her hand as she stumbled up the steep spiral stairway. "Hey steady on there," he said, but they were still holding hands as Cynthia opened a door and said,"Behold the turret room, my most favourite place on the whole estate. Come and look out of the window. That's my cousin's Cessna parked outside the back door, his name is ridiculously pompous, The Hon Montagu de Berg Lilford-Lewis, so we call him Pomps for short".

She gave a giggle as Sinclair watched in fascination as Pomps walked towards the plane. He seemed to be wearing pyjamas. "Just off to get Mum some prawns from Beira for dinner tonight", he shouted up as he swung the propeller. Sinclair gulped and then caught Cynthia's eye, "Actually he is having you on, he is just going down to the coast for a swim," she murmured. 'My God', Sinclair thought 'this is just like Happy Valley in Kenya.'

The young couple leaned over the balcony and watched the plane take off towards the rolling hills of bright green tea-bushes. There was such order and serenity and opulent living. Sinclair felt dazed and heady but this was a magical moment indeed never to be repeated and suddenly they were in each other arms. "Excuse me, what am I doing. Please don't think that I..." Sinclair gasped. He really didn't know what had come over him. How could he be so damn stupid, must be that wine at lunch. Probably ruined his chances now. "Don't be so silly Sinclair, it's the hot Africa sun, gets to you in the end, you're probably a slow starter," Cynthia smiled wickedly. "How about a repeat performance?"

"Where have you been all my life?" whispered Sinclair as he nibbled Cynthia's ear. "Waiting for you Sinclair. I always knew it would happen this way," Cynthia laughed up into his face and ruffled his hair. "Now come on let's go and have a swim."

Afternoon tea was poured out of a Georgian teapot and accompanied by a confectionery of cucumber and Gentleman's Relish sandwiches

TEA ESTATES:
Estate workers picking the three fragrant tea leaves at the top of the plant. Although some of Malawi's most fragrant tea comes from the Nkata Bay area of the country, the industry was first established in the Mulanje/Cholo region with private estates developing this section of the agricultural economy. Tobacco, both flue-cured and sun-dried, have become strong secondary export crops.

and an enormous cream cake.

Sir Giles breezed in from the dam bearing a basket of freshly caught chambo and an unusually nervous Cynthia introduced Sinclair to her rather frightening relative. After giving him a steely 'I think he'll do' look, Sir Giles smiled, handed the fish to Sinclair and ordered him to stay for supper and help eat them. "Got to get to know you my boy. Family's important what? Now tell me about yourself. Where do you work and where are you heading. Ever thought of tea planting? Johanna, you must write to Emmeline and tell her we've met Sarah's sprog." He turned back to Sinclair and slapped him on the shoulder. "By the way young feller, heard anything about this chap Banda? Stirring up the locals I believe, now he wants to take over the country. Not cricket you know."

Sinclair confessed to not knowing much about Dr Banda, but promised to let Sir Giles know further details. "I understand he is quite a highly trained doctor Sir," he added. Sir Giles gave him a quick hard look. "I hope you are not one of those liberals?" "Absolutely not, Sir," Sinclair said hastily and was rewarded with another slap on the shoulder, "That's all right then my boy, come again and soon."

Later that day a dazed Sinclair drove back to Zomba in the cool of the evening. Somehow the sunset seemed more glorious than usual. He waved to the many smiling pedestrians walking on both sides of the mountain road carefully avoiding the swinging baskets of live chickens. Woops, just missed that goat thank goodness. What a wonderful country this is, he murmured. What a lucky chap I am.

Although apparently unable to speak Chinyanja well and always addressing political meetings and rallies through an interpreter, Banda's dynamic personality and almost God-like leadership qualities fired up a national campaign, that culminated in civil disorder and riots in March 1959. The colonial authorities declared a state of emergency, banned the NAC and arrested its leaders. Dr Banda was detained and escorted to Rhodesia where he remained in prison for nearly a year.

CHAPTER FIFTEEN
WEDDING RITUALS

The relationship developed slowly but inevitably, with picnics by the side of ice-cold mountain streams. Once a month they took a trip over the border to enjoy enormous curried queen prawns and chilled wine in a quaint café over the border in Portuguese East Mlanje, followed by a swim in the DC's very green swimming pool, perched on the top of a very steep rocky hill behind his house.

Parties, lunches, dinners, suppers and swimming sessions at midnight took place continuously and amazing friendships developed. Everyone wanted to be a part of their growing love and both Cynthia and Sinclair felt somehow suspended in time. Each day was unique.

Even the arrest of Dr Hastings Banda during the riots in March 1959 and his subsequent imprisonment in Rhodesia had absolutely no impact on the young couple. They had no idea that 1960, the year of their wedding, would herald such change in the country.

The golden months went by, Christmas, New Year and then suddenly it was the day before the wedding with the only stumbling block being Sinclair's Stag Night organised by Jacko. "Now look here Sinclair," Cynthia said sternly over the phone. "I don't want you to drink too much, just watch that Jacko, I have a feeling he has something planned, something nasty, so take care. You and Jacko must be at the Estate guest cottage early in the morning. All your wedding gear will be waiting for you. Darling, I do hope Jacko's speech as best man will not be too close to the bone. Remember all the delicate maiden aunts travelling over from England under the care of both our mothers. Can't have them all fainting in the bushes."

"Worry not, I love you, roll on tomorrow night," said Sinclair unthinkingly. "Hey my boy take everything in the right order, you are supposed to enjoy the wedding day too." Cynthia giggled, "Love you too."

Later that evening Jacko led the blindfolded Sinclair into the Club where twenty or so envious young men greeted him with rousing cheers. They were all on their third beer and ready to go.

"First Sinclair old lad," shouted Jack, "You must quaff the special drink prepared for you by my own fair hand and called Lead in the Pencil." Roars of laughter greeted the name. "Come on open up for Daddy, down the hatch."

"I say Jacko, hold on now." but Sinclair's protestations went unnoticed and he seemed to be swallowing non-stop for five minutes. But once down and warm in the tummy he was soon joining in a mad game of Bok Bok, followed by the traditional Yard of Ale, followed by a wild Zulu dance across the cricket pitch. A swim seemed a good idea but after that Jacko said they had prepared a special bath for the bridegroom. Weak with laughter, it was not until he was plunged into a tin bath that he realised the water was bright green.

"Well, old boy, you are a bit of a greenhorn bridegroom so let's get the colour right." Jacko rolled with laughter as two of the other lads poured more liquid over an almost comatose Sinclair. "Woops lads, I think Sinclair's had enough wild bachelor life to remember for the rest of his married life, let's wash him off and pop him into his bed." Norton, Sandy, Philip and Jacko carried Sinclair to the shower, but try as they could, the dye did not respond to the most vigorous of scrubbing. Sinclair from the neck downwards was as green as a village cricket pitch.

"Bit of a problem here, let's run a bath and pop in a bottle of bleach," Sandy helped lower Sinclair into the water where he slouched for a few seconds before letting out a frightful scream. The bleach had reached some tender places and now the dye was patchy. Sinclair looked like a very poorly camouflaged gamekeeper. "A wode-covered warrior perhaps?" whispered Philip behind his hand.

Jacko gave him a stern look. "That's not funny old man. Now let's tackle this the right way. Do we have to change the body? No, we can cover it," Jacko looked critically at his moaning friend. "The face and head are OK, so while his clothes are on, he'll be OK for the wedding. Pity about the hands, but we can borrow some gloves from the Club waiters. Someone run up to the hospital and get some bandages for his neck."

"But what about poor old Cynthia tomorrow night?" Norton looked aghast at the thought of a spoilt wedding night. They all thought deeply about this. Certainly no one would fancy Sinclair, not even a madly in love wife.

"Well I can handle that," Jacko said confidently "The Vicar's a good fishing friend of mine. I'll ask him to include some powerful stuff in his address to the bride and groom about Cynthia taking him for better or worse. Nothing like a bit of a challenge during those first heady days of marriage."

The next day saw a very pale and subdued Sinclair standing at the altar waiting for his bride. "Take off those terrible gloves," hissed his mother, "and why are you wearing a bandage round your neck?"

The Bridal music began and Sinclair turned to see a vision of beauty floating down the aisle. This will be the shortest marriage in history, he thought to himself miserably. Cynthia raised her eyebrows slightly when he insisted she put his ring on the little finger of his gloved hand. "Is there something you want to tell me darling?" she murmured. Sinclair gave a weak smile.

Somehow the Reception held on the lawns of the Estate passed in a dream. Sinclair could hear laughter, toasts, many congratulations and tears from his mother. He was surprised to find that he managed his speech remembering to thank all the right people but as they drove away to the sound of cheers and clattering tin cans, he thought miserably. How am I going to tell her?

Later, much later, after Cynthia had drawn the curtains on a moonlit night, they lay in a warm bundle of arms and legs. Cynthia nuzzled Sinclair's ear. "Darling I have a confession to make. I know all about the dye. Jacko told me. Said it was a celebration that went a bit wrong. However, much as I love you I would rather not see you bright green on our wedding night, so no lights tonight and do try and pop on your dressing gown before I open my eyes tomorrow morning."

She started to laugh and Sinclair joined in and their laughter rang through the little mountain top hotel making other guests smile as they drank their cocoa and pondered on youthful days and nights of young love.

CHAPTER SIXTEEN
SETTING UP HOME

After the honeymoon Sinclair and Cynthia moved into a house in Misere Farm. It was old, dark, and rather dilapidated but it did have two lovely litchi trees in the garden and three small bedrooms. "There are some lovely ripe litchi on the trees and just think Sinclair, we'll be able to have guests to stay overnight," said Cynthia happily. "However I'm going to need some money to get curtain material from Lulats. I also need pots, pans, dishes, and I'll get some cutlery from Aunt Johanna when we go over next. She's got masses of stuff to spare." Cynthia consulted her list. It was rather long but it was going to be such lovely fun playing house with such a delicious husband.

They toured the house together and discovered that it was already furnished with sturdy PWD furniture. "These old wardrobes must have been left here by Livingstone." snorted Sinclair. "But they are enormous Sinclair, and look at all these little side-drawers. Heavens above this one's lined with a Telegraph dated 1939. Look Sinclair it's the issue announcing the start of the Second World War. I'm going to frame this." Cynthia carefully extracted the brittle paper and put it aside.

They examined the bedrooms more closely. Each contained two modest beds overhung with enormous and well-patched mosquito nets. Sturdy burglar bars framed the windows, which were covered with mosquito gauze. "I'm sure some jolly curtains will cheer up these horrid little rooms", said Sinclair with confidence "But I'm going to ask PWD for a double-bed. No way can we both fit into one of these boarding school singles."

"Come on Sinclair, let's try out that theory." Cynthia jumped onto one of the beds, which creaked alarmingly. She held out her arms and what else could Sinclair do but join her for a cuddle. But as they lay there, enjoying a long and delicious kiss, suddenly the metal frame and mattress gave way under them and locked together they crashed to the floor. "You were right Sinclair", gasped Cynthia. "Maybe mattresses on the floor will be the answer until we get a double."

Extracting themselves with difficulty and much laughter they continued the tour of the house. Two rooms definitely defied change; the kitchen, where a massive and very old-fashioned stove dominated, and the bathroom, which contained a narrow ancient bath scored and marked by years of leaking taps. "Tell you what Sinclair, let's bath by candlelight and put a rose-coloured light-bulb in the kitchen. That way we'll never really see either rooms too clearly." Cynthia whirled Sinclair to his feet and, to the great enjoyment of Yassein the cook, they danced throughout the house to the sounds of Swingin' Safari. "The young Master and Madam are too happy," Yassein confided to Tickey, the gardener. "I think we will like working for this nkosikas."

In the weeks ahead Cynthia's artistic talents touched each room and imposed the very best decor possible under the circumstances, with the sitting room a masterpiece of market baskets and David Whitehead's traditional cloth. "I can't believe that's the same ghastly old lounge suite," gasped Sinclair. "How did you do it, you clever old thing? Not sure about that potty painted over with sunflowers in the loo but if you like it...!"

"Called nouveau art Sinclair, we've got to keep up to date darling," Cynthia called back over her shoulder. "Well as long as you don't spray a bra and hang it in the bedroom." Sinclair dodged the flying cushion as he ran out onto the veranda. "Come on Cynthia let's go over and meet the neighbours."

An hour or so later they were comfortably installed on the stoep of Frikki and Annalize van der Merwe. "Stoep is Afrikaans for veranda Sinclair, calling it that makes us feel it's home from home", explained Frikki with a laugh. "Well where is home in South Africa?" asked Cynthia. "We come from Tweefontein, a farming area in the Transvaal, with seven families, our families by the way, working five thousand morgen of land, mostly cotton and cattle." Frikki continued. "I have come up on contract to help set up a community cotton project and the money will help me buy my own place when I get back to Twee, I think we have done the right thing, but it hasn't been that easy moving out of our small community into Little England". They all laughed but Cynthia thought 'I bet they've been a mite lonely. We must invite them over for supper next week."

Cynthia turned to Annalize, "Tell me Annalize where do you buy your groceries?" I went into that small shop called A1 Supamarkit down near the market and all I could find was some wartime bully beef, porridge oats full of weevils, and when I asked for bird seed, the dear little man behind the counter said "Birdi no come from seedi, he come from picannin eggs." They all roared with laughter and wiping her eyes Annalize said "Let's go over together to Blantyre next week. We usually stock up there once a month and then buy the rest from Mandala's here in Zomba. You'll soon learn the ropes Cynthia, but there's not a great range of products. I believe some people go down to Salisbury by small plane once a month. They stock up for £5 return! Amazingly cheap hey!"

Later that evening as Sinclair and Cynthia sat in the small dining room eating Chicken piri piri a-la-Yassein they heard tremendous rustling in the litchi trees. Sinclair approached the trees cautiously. "Never know darling. It could be a leopard or a python. You stay in the house."

Sinclair grasped one tree trunk and shook it vigorously and to his astonishment, three large male Indians fell out of the tree and, abandoning baskets brimful with ripe litchis, they ran off down the drive.

Sinclair went to the other tree and peering up into the branches found a pair of dark brown eyes looking back at him. "Very sorry young Sir, but traditionally we Patels have been permitted to pick some fruit from these trees each season. You see the trees were planted by our grandfather many moons ago." The good-looking young man made no attempt to climb down and run away. "For heaven's sake, why didn't you just come and ask me for some", Sinclair helped the young Indian out of the tree and into the house. "We can't possibly eat all this fruit. Come in and meet my wife."

Ephrim Patel stayed for an hour or more and Sinclair gained new insight into life in the Indian community of Zomba. He discovered that Ephrim was studying law at Calcutta University and was just back home for the long vacation.

A few days later the young couple accepted an invitation to supper with the Patels, a large and colourful family who all seemed to live together in one large house situated in the lower end of Zomba. "This is where we Indians are allowed to build." murmured Ephrim Patel Senior, "we don't mind really, it's near where we make our money!" Durga Patel rattled her gold bangles as if to emphasise the statement as Ephrim went on, "and every year we send our wives over to India with plenty of gold bracelets. Much easier than bothering with travellers' cheques you know." His eyes twinkled as he handed over a dish of vegetable samoosas. "My wife's cooking is famous throughout the Indian community of Zomba. We are vegetarians you know and tonight Durga only added a little touch of chilli in these samosas." It was a night to remember.

"Not quite the done thing old boy," Ted murmured when Sinclair boasted during the office tea break about the wonderful meal they had enjoyed the night before. "It could mean a bit of a question mark on your record." But Sinclair thought to himself 'I'll keep it low-key but I like Ephrim and I'm certainly going to chose my own friends to share my own free time'.

But he realised he would have to be careful and not talk about the friendship in the office. 'What a pity' he thought. 'I really like the Patels, they're such gentle refined people.'

In 1960 the British Government capitulated and Dr Hastings Banda was deported to the land of his birth where he was greeted by thousands of cheering supporters at Chileka Airport.

CHAPTER SEVENTEEN
CYNTHIA LOOKS FOR WORK

"I'm bored." Cynthia announced to Sinclair one evening. "Do you think I could get a job here in Zomba? I'm really finding the constant round of tennis and tea parties a bit hard to take. Do you know what happened today?" "Throw yourself on the couch and reveal all to your resident psychologist." Sinclair dodged the well-aimed shopping basket and sat down prepared to listen. He could see Cynthia was upset.

"Well you know Muffins Ballantyne is a sort of uncrowned Queen of the Police Camp. Well connected you know. She's asked me several times to play tennis which I managed to dodge because you virtually have to give up a whole day somehow."

"Well today she asked me to come to one of her tea-parties to help welcome a batch of newly arrived Police wives. Poor little darlings, when I arrived today to help hand out the cucumber sandwiches in her massive drawing room, there was Muffins sitting on her throne chair a bit higher than the rest of us and all the little ladies from Cheam, Basingstoke and Little Sudbury Under Weir trying to eat, drink tea and answer Muffins constant questions about their family background all at the same time."

"The new wives were mesmerised. They listened, they looked in wonder at the vast silver trays of sandwiches and cakes but it was all too much on top of the three-week sea journey and train trip up from the Coast with the children either fighting or being sick. Then they had the awful business of trying to settle into a hot little house plonked in the middle of a dusty camp garden. Now they were trapped in the clutches of an intimidating but nevertheless high-ranking police wife. I felt so sorry for them and the nervous rattling of teacups was unbelievable."

"Well when Muffins discovered that none of the new arrivals was worthy of a second invitation she started on the old chestnut of her gallstone operation and when she and Oswald dined with the Royals at Buck House. We were given the menu mouthful by mouthful and what Phil and Liz said in awful detail. I was squirming with embarrassment. But there was a lovely twist at the end of the tale when Muffins turned to one poor girl and asked, "Tell me my dear, have you ever met Her Majesty the Queen"? The poor little thing gazed back in horror and then said slowly and dreamily. "Have I met the Queen? No. No. I.... don't...think ...so."

Sinclair roared with laughter and after a bit Cynthia joined in but she was disturbed by the whole event. "Look Sinclair it was funny but it was sad too. Sad for Muffins, sad for the little Mum, but it was certainly the best put-down of Muffins I've ever witnessed, quite unconsciously done of course, but as you can imagine I laughed and laughed and so that's me finished with Muffins Ballantyne and the Police Camp. If looks could kill I am sure Muffins would have done me in with her gold-plated knitting needles."

Sinclair wiped his eyes. "Wait until I tell the boys at the Club."
"Don't you dare Sinclair." Cynthia's eyes flashed with anger. "I'll

never forgive you if you tell anyone, because Muffins is not all bad. She's really a good old girl, very kind in her own funny way. Ex-Guy's hospital sister and runs a free clinic every Friday for the domestic staff on the Camp. Trouble is she has been a colonial for so long she doesn't know anything about real life in the UK these days. Do you know what she said to me once? She told me to always have a complete outfit ready to slip on at a moment's notice, said it always held her in good stead in India when Oswald phoned up and said he was bringing the Rajah for afternoon tea."

Sinclair laughed again but at the same time he realised that Muffins was another potential casualty of future change. "I wonder how she'll settle back into a Sussex village already awash with Indian Army colonels and enough titles to make the local Women's Institute look like a page from Burke's."

Cynthia continued thoughtfully. "But you know that new Senior Police Officer who arrived last month, Smithers, I think. Well, his wife is always talking about Daddy being Colonel of an army regiment with stories of fun and games at the Aldershot Officers' Mess. Well Johnson at the Army Camp says his father knew her old man and he was only a Sergeant Major. Wonder why she needed to lie in that way?"

"It's the system in the Army and Police, one-upmanship, you've always got to be one ahead," Sinclair thought about the Permanent Secretary's dinner party tonight. "We're all the same, angling for a house a little bit higher up the hill. Palsy walsy with the PS, but you watch to-night, even though it's a private party, woe betide if any Junior member of staff gets tiddly or dares to leave before a Senior member of staff; it will be a Black Mark Bentley. The Civil Service list, commonly called The Stud Book, reigns supreme."

Sinclair gave Cynthia a mock salute but she thought to herself. 'I wonder what is worse, being part of it or not belonging at all. But on the other hand, belonging is really not so bad. Is it?' Cynthia pulled a face at Sinclair and continued, "But seriously Sinclair I must get my teeth into a more worthwhile existence. Do you think there are any jobs going with your outfit?"

Sinclair thought for a bit. He could tell that under the laughter Cynthia was feeling rather depressed. "Tell you what darling, they're bit nervous about husband and wife working in the same department in the Service. Also now that Dr Banda has returned to the country in triumph, apparently thousands of cheering blacks met him at Chileka Airport yesterday, there might be a bit of a hold on hiring local whites. But let's see if there is a special position just for you. Certainly there is a completely separate audio-visual aids production unit opening up. They're planning to run a print shop, radio programmes, design a special mobile information unit and print posters. I know they are going to look for a training officer and someone to run the unit as a whole. You did some art training, why not have a bash at it?"
"What a cheek, did some art training. I'll have you know I studied art and design at St. Martin's School of Art, London. Did a bit of radio work and wrote some scripts too. Do you think I'll have a chance Sinclair? And...now I remember I also did a short course with a Nigerian lecturer on research into visual perception and comprehension at grassroots. Who do I have to go and see?" Cynthia brightened up immediately. "Oh Sinclair I do so hope I can get a job."

"Not go and see someone my darling. Number One step in attempting to become a British Civil Servant is to fill in a form. In fact fill it in, in triplicate, because the chaps overseas have to approve of you first. You get the forms from the Secretariat by the way." Sinclair grinned affectionately at his young wife as she rushed out of the room to change into her best frock, 'wonder how she will settle in as a beautiful female white ant', he thought.

She was just getting into the car when Sinclair remembered an important point. He opened the window and shouted. "Don't forget Cynthia to pull out all the heavies in terms of references, get writing to all those relatives overseas and don't forget details of schools and academic achievements, sports played and I was told a bit of theatrical experience helps." Sinclair smiled to himself and settled back with a second cup of coffee. He was glad he was working at home today. Thinking on it, telling Cynthia about the theatrical experience was a bit over the top, but it was lovely to see his darling girl smiling again. He had a good feeling about the job and he knew she would be good at it.

But it was surprisingly easy and although Cynthia was only offered a local contract as Publications Officer, the salary wasn't bad and the work just up her street.

Soon she had workshops organised and the new studio was a hive of activity with artists and writers working together. During a development meeting Cynthia brought up the suggestion of trying out a mobile puppet theatre built into the back of a Ministry of Information mobile unit. The idea was greeted with enthusiasm, although Origan Kyamba Phiri said that he did not advise using the idea in Lilongwe. "You see, Mrs Brown, they use sort of puppet figures in their traditional rituals, it wouldn't do at all." Soon the art room technicians were skilled at moulding the papier-mache puppet heads over plasticine and they excelled at writing very accurate stories of rural home life and carefully weaving in a development message. Luckily, one of the staff, Simplex Nkandawire, was a good musician and Cynthia helped him work out some catchy jingles to play over the vehicle's loudspeaker system.

Sinclair was really surprised at how quickly Cynthia got into the heart of the project. He heard her singing 'talani fetereza' in the bath and knocked at the door. "Hey what happened to the romantic love?

songs?" She giggled as she came out of the bathroom rubbing her hair with a towel. "Oh Sinclair it's so exciting and worthwhile. We've

CREATING PUPPET HEADS
Artists skilfully shape the puppet head out of plasticine that forms a mould. This is then covered with layers of 'papier mache', dried in the sun, painted and finally sewn onto a glove-costume.

made up jingles on all the seasonal agricultural activities and the villagers just love them. We are playing them on the radio programme every week and it seems the whole of the country is singing Simplex's ditties." She rushed off to dress and get to work. Sinclair took his turn in the bathroom. 'What a miracle that this job turned up just in time' he thought to himself as he patted on the aftershave. 'Well done old man, good thinking especially as my little love seems to be very happy indeed.'

After only one month the first of many shows was on the road and a few weeks later Cynthia drove back from a field trip and joined Sinclair on the veranda for sundowners.

RECORDING THE PLAY FOR THE INFORMATION UNIT
The simple plots are created, written and recorded by the Extension Aids Branch staff.

"I'm really thrilled Sinclair, today's puppet show was such a success and an entire community turned out to enjoy the show. Children, mums, dads, grandparents, aunts and uncles all turned up. It was super." She took a sip of her gin and tonic and continued.

"You know I think it's really important to teach new ideas to the whole family so they each see the message from their own perspective. You see we've created a farmer called Bambo Jomba and he's a bit like Mr. Archer of BBC fame. Quite forward thinking but also makes mistakes. We bring in stories about every member of his family and so different ministries can get an extra benefit out of our message. You know, a spot of news on Education, Health and a few cooking hints and recipes. Bambo Jomba talks about Little

Precious starting school, Granny taking her varicose veins to the clinic and Mums meeting at baby clinics. Now, believe it or not, all those different ministries are giving us some of their publicity budgets. It's great. Of course we add some fun, a bit of slap stick and laughter and it goes down so well."

The glove puppets are operated by the driver of the Information Unit with music and words played over the loudspeakers

Cynthia took another sip of her evening gin and tonic. She felt very content.

In 1961 a series of constitutional conferences followed Dr.Banda's release and Elections were held in August when the Malawi Congress Party won overwhelmingly.

CHAPTER EIGHTEEN
THE VILLAGE WEDDING

"Sinclair, guess what, we've been invited to my driver's wedding, next Saturday morning. You know him Oliver Komanji. Are you able to come?" Cynthia looked up from the enormous card and envelope, which had been hand-delivered to the breakfast table by a picannin. "Sorry old dear but I'm going on a course, golf course actually and I can't let the chaps down. It's the Club Championships. Don't suppose you'll want to go on your own. Send a present and regrets." "But I want to go Sinclair and it's quite near to Zomba at a village on the Palombe Plains. I would really like to see a traditional village wedding. I'll get a map from Oliver." Sinclair was not all that keen on Cynthia travelling through the bush on her own but reassured by her determination and promises to return before dark, he gave his consent. "Be careful what you eat and drink darling, no refrigeration out on the Plains yet."

Next Saturday saw Cynthia setting off with a prettily decorated tea set, suitably wrapped for the bridal couple. "Take some cash too Cynthia," Sinclair shouted as he packed his clubs into the boot of his car. "They rather expect it, look out for the big baskets near the main hut, one side money, the other side presents. Have fun darling and don't forget, come back before dark."

Once Cynthia drove off the narrow tar onto the dirt road she soon realised that the map was quite useless, since the Palombe Plain was crisscrossed with hundreds of small roads and many paths made by both man and cattle. Quite frankly she was lost within a half-an-hour's driving and although the Zomba Plateau was comfortingly evident behind her she was quite relieved to see an old man sitting under a tree, smoking his mealie cob pipe.

"Please can you tell me the way to Kukumbire village?" She asked. The old man looked at her in silence, then he took the pipe out of his mouth, gestured around him and said, "Nkosikas, is this place you seek in this world?"

Cynthia thought about that very carefully. Probably his world was at the most 20 square miles. "No indeed old one, it is not in this world but in a nearby one and today there is a big wedding and I am supposed to be there. Can you help me?". Cynthia looked suitably downcast.

"Ah yes if it is a wedding that you are looking for I can help you, for I, Benjamin Chirwa am senior uncle of the bride and I am also going to the wedding by footing but I needed to rest a while. Perhaps it would be helpful if I sit with you and show the way?" The old man rose to his feet and soon was beside Cynthia directing the route with his pipe. It was surprisingly easy as Benjamin pointed out the small pieces of material and paper tied to trees. "You see Nkosikas, it is quite easy to find the wedding." 'Hope I can find the way back' thought Cynthia.

Soon they saw a bunch of balloons tied to a bush and rounding a corner they found a village bedecked with branches of brightly coloured flowers with all the villagers dressed in their Sunday best.

As Cynthia got out of the car and started towards the main hut where dignitaries were obviously waiting to greet guests, some children rushed to roll down split-cane mats before her. She walked on them with great difficulty as her high-heeled shoes kept sticking in between the slats and soon she was dragging the mats behind her. It was most embarrassing as everyone was watching. Everyone gave a deep sigh as she nearly stumbled. "Aaaah". The sound rose up and down like a gentle wind.

However what made matters worse was as she managed to walk off one mat the children would run behind, roll it up and rush in front of her to spread it out once more. The walk seemed to take forever but she eventually reached the veranda and shook hands with everyone, after placing her gift in a large basket on one side of the door and the money in a basket on the other side. 'Thanks for the tip Sinclair', she murmured to herself.

Soon she was seated in a small individual shade hut obviously built especially for her comfort. A little girl knelt at her feet with a bowl of water and a towel and Cynthia freshened up whilst a variety of food and drink was placed on the small table in front of her. Some fried mopani worms caught her eye at once and could that be a fried locust? 'Help me Lord' she thought.

Everyone was looking at her and yet no one appeared to want to join her in her isolation until she was surprisingly given personalised entertainment by an n'anga, a spirit doctor, often wrongly called a witchdoctor, she remembered Sinclair telling her. He was dressed in the usual rather smelly skins and beads with a head-dress of massive feathers and his main party piece seemed to be inserting safety pins through his arm without any apparent bleeding.

'Could those feathers be ostrich? Cynthia said to herself. She peered closely and saw that underneath all the ancient trappings, he was a good-looking young man. She thought she caught a wiff of Brut deodorant. No it can't be. She thought to herself. However, Cynthia found him a rather entertaining diversion at a wedding ceremony that seemed to be on hold. She smiled her thanks, imagining that he was unable to speak English, however to her astonishment he abruptly gave up the seemingly painless pinning, went and fetched a chair and sat down beside her.

THE VILLAGE WEDDING
Traditionally the country has a matriarchal society and so the bridegroom generally moves to his wife's village. However the family totems still influence the suitability of choice of partners. On the traditional bridal walk from the bridegroom's village the elderly women of the villages jeer and mock the young couple trying to upset them. It is a sort of test on their future endurance of hard time. As you can see the young couple look suitably stern and resolute.

"Name is Misheck Muchena, how do you do, as you British say!" Raising a sophisticated eyebrow, he shook her hand vigorously. "Expect you are wondering what I'm doing here dressed up like this! My father's the local Chief round here and I went to the Secondary School in Blantyre before going down to Fort Hare University to study political science and economics." He explained further. "Then of course, I went over to the UK to do my post-grad." The Oxford accent was extraordinary. "Trouble is the family spirits told my grandfather to hand on the family healing knowledge and ancient bones to me, so technically I'm the local healer. Actually I'm really rather good at it and so I'll continue until Independence, when I hope to get a Government job, in fact I know I'm getting a rather good job. Have you heard the rumour that the British Government has given in and full self-government will be given to the country in the New Year with Kamuzu Banda taking over as Prime Minister in February '63?"

"How do you know all this Misheck." gasped Cynthia. Joseph laughed. "Not much point in being an n'anga if you don't listen to the drums." He winked. "Also having an uncle close to the old man helps and I was involved in the elections, backroom boy of course." He gave a great roar of laughter and Cynthia could not help but join in. She found him a fascinating companion and since natural medicine was one of her pet interests they shared an interesting hour discussing the comparative merits of traditional and Western medicine.

After a while Cynthia looked round and said "I say Misheck, where's the bride and groom?" Misheck went on nibbling the fried mopani worms. "Traditions my dear Cynthia, traditions. Filomina and Olifer are walking from his village to this village, which is Filomina's home. Don't you know that Nyasaland sports a matrilineal society? The traditional husband always joins the traditional wife's community. Look here they come." Misheck pointed to a long line of people dancing their way slowly through the bush.

As they came closer Cynthia could see the bride in a long white dress with a veil of mosquito netting some twenty yards long under which twenty or so children were dancing. It looks rather like the Chinese dragon dance Cynthia thought. The drums were beating, the horns were blowing and the singing voices rose and fell in rhythmic harmony.

"Look Cynthia, watch how the old women running in front of the couple are jeering, trying to make the newly-weds react." Misheck pointed to the bride and groom who kept their eyes downcast and their faces unsmiling. "You see it's a sort of a test, preparation for the life they face together in fact. They must be able to take sorrow and ill-treatment without falling apart."

"Sort of traditional on-the-spot counselling." murmured Cynthia. "Let me tell you how it works", Misheck said firmly. "The Little Mother, who is usually an aunty on the mother's side plays an important role in arranging the marriage and agreeing the labolo, that's the bride price. Little Mother is always the first one to know if there is trouble between a couple and she has to listen to their problems, advising them on how to build a happy relationship. Mostly it works. The only valid reason for divorce is if the bride cannot produce children. Believe it or not in the old days being barren was a legitimate reason for suicide, but then many men had two or three wives just to make sure of an heir..." Cynthia interrupted him. "But I heard Misheck that if a man dies leaving a wife and children, the wife is forced to become a second wife for a living brother, it seems so ghastly and heartless."

Misheck shook his head. "No Cynthia not forced, but it is seen as an acceptable solution to a human tragedy. It may not be what the widow wants out of life Cynthia, but look at it this way, who else in the family should or could look after her and the children. With no education, or job, what are the alternatives? How would she and the children survive? Her family wouldn't have them back. You see, the age-old traditional system provides for survival. It may not be your kind of survival but it certainly worked in the past in this country. Now it's more difficult with modern educated wives working, earning their own money and being independent. In a way they've buggered up the system."

They talked on and on, oblivious of the lively party developing around them. 'What a pity it is that more is not known of these old traditional ways of life in this country' thought Cynthia. 'I do hope these gentle customs will not be lost in the excitement of Independence'.

As the bridal couple came towards the maternal parent's hut the wedding cake, all three glorious tiers in position, was carried out in triumph. It was a masterpiece of white confectionery. Cynthia watched in horror as three chickens chased by a dog ran in front of the cake bearer who slipped and fell to her knees. The top layer of the cake complete with figurine of bride and groom wobbled and fell to the ground to the sound of a hundred or more 'eeeeeeyaaaah'. There was a breathtaking silence during which time a brave guest picked up the pieces and calmly pushed cake and icing together again. And if the top layer was rather red-dust-coloured, nobody seemed to worry. Everyone clapped. The wedding had begun. Let the dancing begin.

Just before dark Cynthia arrived home to find Sinclair waiting anxiously for her. "Are you alright darling. I was getting a bit worried you know." She gave him a long hug. "Oh Sinclair it was so lovely and I am so glad I went. Let me tell you all about it over a g and t."

CHAPTER NINETEEN
SINCLAIR THE GARDENER

"I say darling, I do think you ought to take a bit more of an interest in the garden," Cynthia stood in the kitchen doorway and threw her gardening gloves at Sinclair who caught them expertly. She continued. "I'm going away to set up the Lilongwe Agricultural Show stand next week, so how about taking over my Adam the gardener's spot. Ticky's great on digging but he doesn't know much about cuttings and our kind of vegetables. How about it? You are supposed to be the agriculturist of the family you know!"

"Nothing to it old dear." said Sinclair with a wave of his beer. "Would you like me to organise mushrooms, artichokes, perhaps?" Cynthia threw her gardening hat at him. "Just keep the garden going darling and spinach and carrots will do."

However when next Monday arrived and Ticky stood at the backdoor awaiting his early morning instructions, Sinclair was at a bit of a loss. He looked round the garden thoughtfully. "Here's what you do Ticky. Make a new vegetable bed here. Then let the ducks out of the pen for a bit and let them scratch in that old vegetable bed. Then wash out their house and pour the manure on the new veggie bed and the compost heap. Oh yes and by the way plant these pumpkin seeds in the compost heap."

Sinclair handed Ticky a packet of seeds and went off to his car whistling the Archers radio programme theme song. 'Running a garden. Nothing to it' he thought. But Ticky looked puzzled. 'Eeee, there were too many orders. Now what was the first thing to do!' He scratched his head and knew it was going to be a bad day.

Sinclair popped into the Club for a toot or two after work. All his pals were there and after all Cynthia was away and probably living it up in Lilongwe so he dallied an hour or so. After all he knew that she had organised a daily menu for him so when he arrived home he was surprised to find Ticky huddled by the back door. "What's wrong Ticky? Are you sick?" he asked.

Ticky seemed to have difficulty in speaking but eventually he croaked out. "Eee, Master, it has been a terrible day. I did all that you asked but it was too hard. I have not rested, I have not eaten, I am about to die."

Sinclair thought back and wondered what could have gone wrong. "Tell you what, let's go round the garden and see where things went wrong." By the light of a torch Sinclair noted the well-washed duck pen and the old and new veggie beds, primed with fresh manure. But when he arrived at the compost heap he recoiled in horror. There buried up to their necks in soil were twelve angry ducks. The soil had obviously been stamped down hard around their necks and they were unable to do more than open and shut their beaks.

"Good heavens man, how did you get them to stay like that?" gasped Sinclair. "Aaaaaa Boss it was too hard, I had to feed them one by one, with those tiny seeds you gave me but the ducks were too cross with me. It was too hard but I did everything just as you said." Ticky looked on the point of tears.

There was a moment of horrified silence and then Sinclair began to laugh. He laughed and laughed until his eyes were streaming with tears, "Ticky, old lad, I did not want you to do this. Didn't you think that it was a funny thing to do?" Sinclair collapsed on the garden bench.

"Oh yes Master," Ticky replied with dignity. "I thought it was a very strange thing to do but then all you Europeans are strange. You ask us to do many strange things. Many of us think that you Europeans are quite mad."

Sinclair looked at the old man and saw the tiredness in his eyes and immediately felt humbled by his gardener's words. "Yes you are right my friend, there are times when I do not understand you and you do not understand me. I guess we'll just have to try a bit harder. Come on, come and have a cup of tea and something to eat, the Madam left plenty of food for us, but let's get the ducks back in their house first."

The evening sun settled over the house as the ducks waddled back to their pen angrily shaking their dirty feathers, and Sinclair and Ticky sat on the back veranda and drank their tea thoughtfully. Nothing more could be said. It was the end of rather an unusual day. A lesson had been learnt.

CHAPTER TWENTY
BUILDING A JETTY

"Sinclair, would you mind driving up to Mangoche next week and help supervise the building of a jetty for the new Fisheries Institute. You know, look at it from an environmental point of view." Ted had breezed into Sinclair's office, where his Number Two Officer was working on an article on Community Self-Help for Farm News. "Be glad to Ted, if only to get away from this article. I'm really struggling." He tossed the draft over to his superior who, after reading it, said, "Sorry old lad, but you haven't quite got the idea. Tell you what, come with me tomorrow and inspect my latest self-help project. Remember I told you that after the successful bridge building, we felt we should build on the first success story, so we asked the same villagers what they wanted next, and they said a community hall. They have already commenced work and are getting on really well, so why not come and have a look see with me tomorrow. It will give you a better idea of the concept and how it works. The enthusiasm of the villagers is a real inspiration. Are you free?"

The next day saw the two of them sitting side by side on a fallen tree watching a most extraordinary and very busy scene. An entire village from the oldest to the youngest members of the community appeared to be involved in constructing a large building.

SELF-HELP SCHEMES:
Self-help played a major role in the development of post-Independence Malawi. It took several years to persuade these villagers that building a bridge over a seasonal river would improve their quality of life. Once agreed, the bridge was built by hand in a couple of weeks. The villagers turned the project into a musical occasion with the women providing food for a celebration party.

Ted turned to Sinclair, and pointed to a bridge behind them. "Look there Sinclair, and you will understand that the women are community motivators at grassroots in Nyasaland. We talked for a couple of years or more to the men but in the end, we really sold the idea of the bridge to the women because they saw the practical benefit. They would be able to get to the shops, take sick children to the clinic and sell their vegetables at the market. Now the whole community is falling over itself for more change. They are really ambitious and lets face it, a community hall will benefit the whole community, men, women and children! Already the women are talking about a pre-school class, a sewing club and the men are keen to make tables and chairs so that they can hold meetings and family functions, like a wedding. It will be a good way of making some money for the next project." He passed a cool drink to Sinclair and pointed to each of the different groups, "Look how well they are all working together."

The two men watched as one team of men made bricks out of mud and laid them out to dry in the sun. Another team was moving enormous rocks and logs in rhythm to the beat of a drum. Even the mixing of the mud, or dagga as it is called, had a dance-like hypnotic quality to it. In the distance singing women were clearing the land to establish a vegetable garden, their powerful voices rose and fell in natural harmony and soon the men joined in. It was a magical moment for Sinclair and he too became caught up in the excitement of the project. Yes, he could see it clearly now. It was not just about building a tangible structure; it was about building a dream for the future.

"Ted, I want to go back and write it up before I lose the feel of today." The day was drawing to a close as the two men shook hands with all the village elders and drove off down the dusty road to Zomba. Ted kept quiet on the drive home. He could see that Sinclair was really impressed by the success of the project and perhaps emotionally charged up by the way in which the whole

community worked together.
"Think you have enough information to write that article?" Ted asked as he dropped Sinclair back home. Sinclair looked at his boss with greater respect. "Ted I feel really humbled by these villagers. It's a beautiful simple story of people who believe in their ability to improve life in the community. I tried to complicate the story too much before. Thanks for putting me right." Next morning saw Sinclair sitting at his desk. He put a clean sheet of paper into the typewriter and shamelessly began to type the headline of his article. '*Self help, a simple, effective way to fulfil a community dream in Nyasaland.*'

'Thanks Ted,' he murmured under his breath, 'I owe you one.' Later that week, Sinclair sat at his desk and decided he was very bored. He wondered why he had not heard about the trip to Mangoche. Maybe it had been cancelled! It was coming up to the rains and so it was oppressively hot, and since most of the staff had taken leave to prepare their home farms for planting as soon as the rains broke, little was going on in the office. Sinclair gave a deep sigh. Even the postal service from the UK had dried up so there was no cheery letter from mother.

'Perhaps I'll book a spot of leave and take Cynthia up to the Farmers Marketing Board cottage at the Lake,' he pondered. Suddenly the telephone jangled, 'I wonder if it's the PS ringing about my promotion' but instead a familiar Irish voice shouted down the line. "Hello there me boyo." It was Paddy O'Flynn from the Public Works Dept. Mangoche. Sinclair smiled to himself as he remembered past escapades and parties with the laughing man from Kerry described by Jacko as 'someone who might fit into the jolly old Emerald Isle but working within the Colonial Civil Service yardstick, I'd say Paddy seems as nutty as a fruit cake.'

'Now here is a real picture book Irishman if ever there was one,' Sinclair smiled, remembering some of their previous escapades, but

Paddy interrupted. He seemed anxious. "Wondered if you were busy Sinclair old lad, I need a spot of agricultural advice and a shovelful of support on a wee project. Can you come up for a day or two?" Paddy roared down the phone which was giving off splutters and hisses like a boiling kettle. "Love to come," roared back Sinclair "May I bring Cynthia?" "Splendid idea me man and bring a drop of poteen. Hang on a minute I think Brigid wants something too."

Paddy relayed the grocery list to Sinclair and later that afternoon the young couple set off down the long dusty road to the Lake. It was a glorious day and as they drove along the dirt road running between the Zomba mountain range and the Palombe Plains the dust rose high behind them. Streams of people walking in both directions waved them on their way and chickens, goats and dogs scattered in all directions as they drove through the almost continuous villages.

"Often wonder where all these people are walking to," commented Sinclair. "But you know Cynthia I'm a bit worried about the Liwonde ferry these days. It's so old and really should be replaced by a bridge. One day there's going to be one hell of an accident." Sinclair wrinkled his brow and then laughed. "Did you hear about old Fothergill Jones getting swept down the river at Ngwezi?" "No," giggled Cynthia. "What on earth happened"? "Well, apparently it was one of those old ferries pulled by a team of men. The ropes were ancient of course and this particular day the rope broke and the ferry just floated down the river for about twenty miles. Old Fothergill had to walk back up the river followed by goats, chickens, dogs and some twenty-five villagers. Took them about six hours. Must have looked like Exodus a la Nyasaland."

They both laughed at the mental picture of old Fothergill Jones with his sunburnt knees and ginger handlebar moustache. "I'm surprised he actually knew which direction to walk, terrible sense of direction has old Foth." Sinclair drove onto the ferry and continued. "I expect he got plenty of advice from the locals but you know it could have been very nasty, plenty of crocs and hippo in that river. Anyway I'm going to keep my eyes on the ferry today." But they crossed safely and eventually arrived at the enchanting little lakeshore town of Mangoche and drove up towards Paddy's house through palm trees quivering with monkeys.

LIWONDE FERRY ON THE SHIRE RIVER:
Water is a great meeting place in Africa, not just for washing clothes and bodies but also to cool off after a hot summer's day.

Sinclair continued. "Remarkable people up here in Mangochi, Cynthia. This little town (used to be called Fort Johnston) was on the direct slave-trading route so there's a strong Arab influence. You can see the inter-breeding in their proud bearing and fine features and they still run veranda or khondi schools from their houses. Can you believe it they write the local language in Arabic form! It was a hell of a job producing literature for them a couple of years ago." Cynthia interrupted him. "Sinclair, it almost sounds as if you admire the Arabs but they were awful to the Africans. Packing them into slave ships, half of them died on the journey and the other half were sold into slavery in America." There was a moment of silence while Sinclair negotiated the car round a pack of dogs racing across the road after a chicken.

"Of course they were awful to the people of Africa but let me tell you something that's not generally acknowledged, the African chiefs and headmen of villages actually worked with the slave-traders and sold their own people to the Arabs. So who were the real criminals?"

Sinclair continued, "...and in fact the Arabs were quite happy to inter-marry and you can see the result very clearly in Mangoche. They also handed on a lot of good advice too, even though it evolved out of their strict religious beliefs." Sinclair waved his hand to a group of fine-featured young men talking on a street corner. They waved back. "Don't let the subject of slavery spoil this special weekend my love," Sinclair gave Cynthia a quick hug. "These breaks from the office are rare these days."

They drove past the Club. "Did I ever tell you that there's an old waiter at the Country Club who remembers meeting Livingstone as a young boy. God knows how old he must be." Sinclair continued "and apparently the Club is affiliated to the British Royal Naval Club. It came about from a gesture of gratitude from some naval bigwig who nearly drowned in the Lake and was saved by a Club member. Can't remember the full details but I'm sure Paddy will tell us the story, he's been here for years."

The minarets of the mosque shone bright pink in the glorious sunset, which also lit up the red sails of the dhows, as they glided across the glassy rose-gold waters of the Lake. "Another legacy from the Arabs."Sinclair commented.

But Cynthia refused to rise to the bait. Regardless of the dust she wound down the window. It was all too beautiful. Fish eagles cried in triumph as they snatched fish from the river running through the historic town. Nearby someone was plucking an mbira, the African harp. It was a magical moment.

"We are so lucky to live in this country Sinclair." Cynthia murmured, "Just imagine I might have been quite content with Spain once a year if I'd stayed in England." She gave a deep sigh of contentment.

A noisy welcome awaited them at Paddy's and later that evening after joining in bedtime games with young Liam and Shelagh, Paddy briefed Sinclair on tomorrow's work. "You'll be knowing about the new Fisheries Institute. Well it seems that the Director Alfred Nooks, who is now running the place, wants a proper tie-up jetty for his boat. He's a bit of an odd boyo if ye wants me opinion. Invited me to lunch with him one day and gave me one sardine on toast. Great Saint Patrick, can you imagine me having lunch without me potatoes." Paddy bent double with laughter. "Anyway, Sinclair we'll be setting off at the crack tomorrow and Brigid and Cynthia can make up a picnic for us. Nice thick ham sandwiches eh me boy!"

The next day the two friends set off up the winding road to the Fisheries Institute. Paddy pointed to the sign saying 'Beware of elephants". "You'll know of course that no one's seen a jumbo here since the 1920s but the sign's still bravely flying. I'll say this for you English, me man, you're bloody persistent. Good for tourists of course."

"What tourists," asked Sinclair? "Ah weel, we can live in hope me boyo," Paddy gave a grin. "I did see one visitor last year. He stayed at the hotel and found a rather nasty snake in his bed and then Hilda, that tame hippo, looked in through his bedroom window and the poor old devil promptly had a heart attack, rotten publicity hey!"

They travelled along the very rough and bumpy road in companionable silence until Sinclair asked idly "Where's the dynamite Paddy?" There was a brief silence as Paddy swerved to avoid a chicken. “In the boot me boy.” Paddy indicated with a backward flick of his head.

A few more miles went under the wheels before Sinclair turned, and looking at the backseat, said nervously, “But Paddy where are the detonators?”

“In the boot too of course, well wrapped up. Nothing to worry about.”Paddy started to sing something about ‘Here’s to Ireland undivided’ but Sinclair wasn’t listening. The final five miles were like something out of a film he’d once seen called ‘Wages of Fear” and any moment he expected to be blown to glory.

But the luck of the Irish prevailed and they arrived at the lakeshore and together with the Fisheries Director and staff examined the enormous rock, which was to be flattened and fitted with an iron ring. The new Institute constructed above the shoreline and surrounded by palms, glistened with new paint. It stood proud and expectant. The ‘day of the jetty’ had arrived and a large crowd of locals joined the Fisheries staff to watch proceedings.

With a great deal of laughter and banter, holes were drilled in the rock and explosives set in place. Everyone retired to a safe place out of range of the big bang. Woooof! The sound was deafening and there was a chorus of Eeeeeeees and Ahaaaaaas from the watching blacks. The working party went forward to examine the very small depression that had been made on the top of the boulder. Behind them the glass windows of the new Fisheries Institute slowly cracked and fell to pieces. There were more Eeeeeeees and respectful sighs from the watchers. This was indeed great European magic and entertainment.

“We’ll have to double the charge boyos and re-angle the bloody holes to shield the building.” Paddy, looked anxious, trying to display confidence that he did not feel, whilst he and Sinclair drilled more holes and packed in the charges. "There, that'll do it." he patted the boulder as if to say, 'Behave yourself you little rascal'. Again everyone retired, somewhat further back than before, and settled down for the explosion. Wooooooooof!! and this time a thin slice of the boulder fell to the ground as the ceilings of the Fisheries Institute crashed majestically to the floor.

The watching staff and villagers melted away into the bush because they could see that the Director was almost incoherent with rage. He was also very fearful of Head Office retribution, as the Permanent Secretary had made it quite clear he thought the work was unnecessary. How would he take the news of the virtual destruction of the new building? He ran into his modest house, which stood behind the Institute, locked the door and refused to come out. "Go away you bloody mad Irishman." he roared through the door, "You've ruined the Institute".

PALM BEACH, FORT JOHNSTON: *(now called Mangochi)*
One of the first hotels built on Lake Nyasa. Golden sands, warm waters and wonderful chambo fishing made it a very attractive holiday centre.

Paddy called back in a deceptively gentle voice. "Don't be getting into a lather Mr. Nooks. Sure we can fix up the windows and ceilings in no time at all, at all." He listened at the keyhole and then peered through. Alfred seemed to be lying on his stomach bent on tearing his pillow in two. Sinclair tried to make contact too.

"Look Mr. Nooks there's no point in continuing with the jetty exercise. "I'm afraid the rock's too hard. We're going to tie a large heavy rope around the boulder and you can use that to secure your boat until we can plan something else. Maybe you could set up a one-day seminar to explore possibilities? Do you agree?" Sinclair's words seemed to send Alfred into an even greater frenzy.

Sinclair looked at Paddy and Paddy looked at Sinclair and they started to laugh. They laughed and laughed until they fell over and lay in a small ditch. Soon a group of locals stood in a respectful ring around them. They pondered upon the laughing men. 'Eeeeee, these Europeans have a strange way of enjoying themselves. Why do they build a house only to enjoy knocking it down by magic!

"Come on Sinclair," said Paddy. "Let's leave the poor old bugger to get over it. How about going off to Palm Beach Hotel for a couple of beers before we eat our sambos!"

And one beer led to two and three and four and as local residents drifted in to hear the story of the jetty, Paddy and Sinclair were treated to more and more beer. Soon a party developed. Midnight saw the car making a very uncertain journey back to Paddy's house. The singing of 'I'll take you home again Kathleen' by Paddy and Sinclair floated through the still air as they passed unsteadily through silent villages. The village headman raised his head from his mat and thought sleepily 'Europeans are mad but I must find out more about their magic, maybe it can remove that anthill in my mealie patch.' and contented with his decision he fell asleep once more.

Full self-government was attained in January 1963 and Dr Hastings Kamuzu Banda became Prime Minister in February of that year.

CHAPTER TWENTY ONE
BREAK A LEG

Sinclair and Cynthia soon became active and useful members of the various sporting sections of the Club but they were a little cautious about joining the Theatre Club, despite past theatrical experiences, and for two very good reasons.

Firstly, from Sinclair's point of view, rather too many high-ranking Civil Service members were active players so Sinclair felt that productions might be rather stuffy affairs. Secondly, Cynthia thought that the permanent producer was much too bossy. "Crumbs Sinclair, I know she's ex-RADA but I've watched a few rehearsals of the panto and Aimee Barker is something else. She seems to lose her rag at the slightest thing. Quite frankly she terrifies me but I would love to have the chance to dance again one day."

But that day came sooner than expected because the leading dancer fell off her horse and broke her leg. "What the devil do you think you're doing ruining my show," Aimee demanded of Joan Levitt as she came round from the anaesthetic. "Why not ask Cynthia Brown to take my place," Joan whispered weakly, tears rolling down her cheeks.

"Now then, stop that blubbing, sorry old thing but it's your own fault. Cynthia Brown you say? Do I know the girl? I'll ask Frederick about her background." By now Aimee was on her feet and ready to investigate an alternative leading lady. "Whoops, nearly forgot, here's a book and some chocolates." She reached the door and with a whirl of her full skirt performed a classic exit. "Cheers for now Joan. Another show! another year perhaps!"

Cynthia was having a quiet cup of tea when Aimee drove her ancient Bentley through the gateway. There was no time to hide, and within a very short time Cynthia found that she had agreed to take over the role of Cinderella. "It was like being mesmerised by a snake," she told Sinclair later. "Guildhall-trained you say? Aimee looked thoughtful. "Well let's see what you can do. Come to rehearsals tonight at seven sharp."

Soon Cynthia was well into the lead role and a small part was found for Sinclair in the chorus and as December approached, rehearsals were held nightly. The first of five performances in Zomba was scheduled for December 15th and it was rumoured that the Limbe Club had requested a Gala night on Christmas Eve. "How are we going to organise Christmas lunch," groaned Sinclair. "Don't worry about that darling, said Cynthia brightly, "I forgot to tell you, Aimee's invited us to her place for Christmas dinner and Aunt Jo wants us over in Cholo on Boxing Day, she's planning a massive party."

Surprisingly Sinclair found that although at least three quarters of the cast were senior to him they were relaxed and friendly. In fact, as he told Cynthia over a late night cup of cocoa, "They're bloody good fun. Did you see old Logan Longdale doing a silent take-off of Aimee in the tea- break? He captured her every gesture, it was hilarious."

"I am sure Logan could have taken up acting as a career." Cynthia said thoughtfully. " Although he is fat, he's just right as the Dame. He somehow exaggerates every move and brings an extra dimension of fun into the panto. He's a magnificent dancer too, so light on his feet. I find it difficult not to laugh myself when we do that pas de deux in the kitchen scene. But did you see how gracefully he landed

SALAD DAYS,
A Zomba Gymkhana Theatre Club production.

when he fell off the stage? That takes some doing when you're built like a hippo." She paused and took another sip of her cocoa. "Oh by the way Sinclair, I've got to go over and help Liz Harmister with her steps tomorrow evening. She's that new girl with the fantastic figure, was Miss Newcastle I believe."

Sinclair opened his eyes. He was nearly fast asleep. "I've met her husband, Joe, nice chap but somehow I don't think their marriage is all that secure. He's really worried at having to leave her in Zomba on her own tomorrow when he goes to do a week's audit in Lilongwe and I don't think he was worried about burglars, if you know what I mean."

Cynthia thought about the situation. "Come to think of it, I was a bit surprised when we were sitting backstage having a gossip when that sexy PWD mechanic Vic Mobbs came past carrying some flaps. Liz went into a sort of 'here I am waiting' mode. Turned sideways to show off her magnificent bust and then fluttered her eyelashes like mad. Old Victor certainly looked at her with a knowing air. I wonder..."

The next night Cynthia knocked on the front door of the Harmister's Blackwood Box. She had not been able to warn Liz of her arrival but knowing Joe was away she took the chance of finding Liz in.

The door swung open and there was naked Liz wrapped in a towel and glowing from a hot bath. The air was heavy with the smell of bath salts and talc.

"Oh sorry to greet you like this, I was expecting... I mean I wasn't expecting visitors. Come in and I'll pop on my robe and we can go over the steps." Liz led the way into the small sitting room.

Soon they were busy working on the chorus dance routine. "I envy you those long legs Liz," Cynthia said with a sigh as they practiced high kicks. " How on earth do you ever get stockings long enough to fit you?" "My Joe gets them from America for me." Liz gave a kick that nearly reached the ceiling. At that moment there was a knock at the door.

"Goodness who could that be?" Liz gave a rather artificial laugh as she went to the front door. "Hallo Victor, what brings you here? Cynthia and I are just going through the dance routine." Liz led a bewildered Vic into the room. He was carrying a bottle of wine and a box of chocolates. He looked cross and Cynthia thought to herself, 'this chap's got a bit of a mean streak in him, he gave poor old Dave Broughton a black eye just for arguing with him about the result of the Cup Final.' But she smiled and greeted him pleasantly. Liz fled to her bedroom and came back wearing a tracksuit and somehow Vic was bundled back out of the front door.

Liz was strangely silent when the rehearsals resumed and when recounting the incident to Sinclair later Cynthia said she thought that Liz had handled it all very well under the circumstances. "Had a bit of practice I guess," said Sinclair thoughtfully. "But I don't think it's over yet,"

Several weeks later Sinclair and Cynthia were just falling off to sleep when there was an urgent knock at their bedroom window. Opening the curtains Sinclair found the distraught face of Joe Harmister looking in. "Please can I come in and talk to you, I'm desperate. I feel like doing myself in."

Several hours and pots of tea later Sinclair and Cynthia had heard the whole sad story of deceit, lies and infidelity. This time he had come back to find them both in bed together, his bed. "I feel like ending it all," he wept, "I love her so but she's bad, really bad." Somehow Joe was persuaded not to end it all and was given a stiff brandy before being tucked away in the spare bedroom. He was exhausted and fell asleep at once though Cynthia heard him calling out in his sleep.

"Poor old bugger," Sinclair said as he settled back to bed at 4am. "It isn't always the men you know Cyn." Cynthia leaned over and kissed him on the nose. "And I know how lucky I am. But don't you ever try anything, my darling, because I'll fight tooth and nail to keep you." Sinclair smiled sleepily as he put his arms around his lovely wife. "I must remember to keep all teeth and every nail locked away for ever then." The cockerel next door crowed loudly and a streak of sunrise swept across the sky. "Don't let's bother with sleep Sinclair we've got an hour left, let's use it creatively." Cynthia giggled and peeled off her nightie.

Weeks later Liz and Victor fled into the night and Joe eventually left Nyasaland to work in the Middle East, where he died of a heart attack at thirty-six years old. "Poor old sod," said Sinclair. "Poor Liz too, Vic left her and she's dying of breast cancer in the UK." Cynthia gazed across the breakfast table at Sinclair. "Life does have a way of paying one back Sinclair."

On 31 December 1963 the hated Federation of Rhodesia and Nyasaland was dissolved.

CHAPTER TWENTY TWO
THE WHITE ANTS MULTIPLY

"Guess what Sinclair I'm preggers and I'm not feeling that good." Cynthia ran for the bathroom and Sinclair lay back in bed. He was still half-asleep but he could have sworn that Cynthia said she was pregnant. Must have been dreaming. But then he heard unmistakable sounds from the bathroom. It must be true. He jumped out of bed and ran to help Cynthia who was feeling ghastly as she vomited down the lavatory.

He put his arms around her and blurted out what seemed to be a whole lot of nonsense to her. Don't be bloody silly Sinclair, how did it happen for heaven's sake. I didn't tell you before now because I wanted to make quite sure. Must have been that night, you know, the night of Joe." Cynthia pale-faced and red-eyed glared up at her husband. "I thought you'd be furious because of, how did you put it! 'Getting ourselves financially established." She was close to tears.

"Darling, it's lovely news. I thought we ought not to start a baby because you were enjoying your job so much." Sinclair wiped her face gently. "Get back to bed and I will tell the office you've got a gippy tummy." Soon everyone in Zomba knew about the Brown baby and knitting needles started clicking all over the town. "It is amazing Cynthia, even the PS asked me how you were doing. Said to tell you to put sticky plasters behind your ears to stop the morning sickness. Apparently it helped his wife tremendously." But nothing helped Cynthia and within a week or two she was on bed-rest and a drip in the top hospital.

"If you go on vomiting like this, you're going to lose this child," the Government Doctor Giles Forester said sternly, Cynthia thought grimly 'Do I have a choice!' However, she was quite happy to lie in a cool breezy room, overlooking the Palombe Plains and wonder about the child within her. 'I wonder if it's a boy or girl?' she thought dreamily. She watched the drip going plop, plop down the narrow tube. It hypnotised her into a refreshing sleep.

"Come on Duckie, time for a nourishing little snack." the elderly Cockney housekeeper, Mabel Clark, gently nudged Cynthia awake and laid an enticing tray of food on the bed. "Oh I couldn't Mabel I really couldn't," protested Cynthia. But Mabel was very firm and feeling rather like a schoolgirl in the Sanatorium under Matron's eagle eye, Cynthia obediently sat up and tasted the tiny portions of delicious food.

"Look, I got you some wild honey, chilled mango and fresh orange juice." Mabel put her arm round Cynthia. "Once you start eating properly and sleeping again dearie, you'll get your strength back."

Mabel sat down on the bed. "Would you like me to chat for a while?" Remembering the day before, Cynthia thought, 'do I have a choice? However, Mabel was such a kind person and her stories, which were quite difficult to unravel, helped to while away the hours before visiting time.'

Yesterday's session began with, "Did I ever tell you about 'Ebert, me 'usband who was in the 'uzzars?" It was difficult not to laugh. Today it was "Did I ever tell you about the time I 'opped along to Mandala's for me groceries and found a family of lions lying on the front doorstep? Only had a copy of Women's Own so I shooed them away with that."

'Mabel obviously survived the big cat encounter, no surprise if she had told them a story, because they would just fall asleep,' Cynthia thought as she drifted off again into a dreamless sleep. Mabel was quite the best sleeping pill she had ever taken.

Mabel was right, the eating and sleeping routine snapped back into place, and soon Cynthia was back home and at work once more. The weeks and months flew by and although her mother was very anxious for her to go back to Britain to have the baby, Cynthia was adamant and made it quite clear on one of her monthly telephone calls. "No Mama, Sinclair and I want to have the baby here in Nyasaland and I want Sinclair with me when I have it. I've got the latest book on easy childbirth and he is learning how to help me with puffing and blowing exercises to control the labour pains. How do you feel about that?"

Sinclair was actually rather uncertain about the whole thing but he hid his fears and agreed to help her. 'After all' he thought, 'It is my baby too.'

The office gave Cynthia a lovely farewell party although the studio head Frank Charters extracted a promise from her to take on free-lance work at home whilst the baby was small. "Come on Cynthia, the little blighters are supposed to just sleep and eat for the first few months, not so?"

However, nature plays tricks on those who make too many forward plans and when she went into premature labour eight weeks early, Cynthia was whisked over to Queen Elizabeth's Hospital, Blantyre where she was given an emergency caesarean section. The Indian surgeon was horrified when she asked for a bikini cut. "What is a bikini cut Mrs Brown?", he whispered softly, but Cynthia was too heavily sedated to explain. "You tell him Sinclair and tell him too I want you with me all the time." But Sinclair was banned from the operating theatre and it was only when he saw a sister hurrying out with a small mewing bundle that he realised the operation was over.

"Lovely little girl, Mr. Brown." she called out "But rather small. We're popping her into the incubator for a while. Have a quick look." The sister pulled back the cloth and showed Sinclair the tiny tranquil face of his daughter. It was love at first sight.

Soon Cynthia was back in the ward and eventually awoke to find Sinclair by her side. He was unwashed and unshaven. "You look terrible," she said sleepily. "You look marvellous, my darling wife, and our daughter is perfectly beautiful." Sinclair gave her a big hug and kiss. "Thanks darling for being such a brave girl."

The next week was a whirl of visitors, flowers and presents for the baby, but the biggest disappointment was that the doctor said that Victoria would have to stay in hospital in Blantyre until she was 5lbs in weight. "But she's only just under 3lbs, it will take ages." Cynthia burst into tears. "Why can't she come to Zomba hospital?" She gazed down at Victoria all wired up and lying inside a small box with an electric light bulb, saucer of water and oxygen pipe. "Can't we take her over in this box? It's not a proper incubator is it?"

"I'm sorry Mrs Brown but you see the facilities are just not there in Zomba. Here we have a proper maternity unit with special nurses to deal with emergencies." Dr. Chandi looked embarrassed at Cynthia's tears. "But you will have to arrange to send over your breast milk in a cold bag every day, the sister will show you how to express it. Perhaps your husband could try and find somebody to bring the bag over."

It seemed an insurmountable problem until a local reporter heard the story. "Can I do a write-up and see if we can get some volunteers?" he asked Sinclair. "Do what you can as quickly as you can," said Sinclair. The response was tremendous, but the final choice was the British High Commission courier who drove daily from Zomba to Chileka airport with the diplomatic bag strapped to his wrist.

For two months, he collected the cold bag from Cynthia and delivered it to the Queen Elizabeth Hospital. "Damned if I expected to end up as a milkman when I joined the Diplomatic Service," laughed John Linden-Jones. "Especially delivering a very specialised brand of milk and having to post a daily bulletin on Victoria's progress on the Club notice board." The story spread to Britain and retired diplomats discussed the matter with barely concealed horror over lunch at the East India Club. "Wouldn't have happened in my day, wives always came home for childbirth. Damn stupid story."

At last the great day came when Sinclair and Cynthia went over to pick up their daughter and take her home. "When Victoria's christened, we'll have the biggest party ever seen in Zomba. It's about the only way we can say thank you to everyone." Sinclair gave his wife and daughter a hug and a kiss. "I must be the luckiest man alive."

Sinclair thought in hindsight that they should have added a traditional name to Victoria Emmeline, because the week of the christening coincided with the celebrations of the birth of Malawi on July 6th 1964. "What about adding Malawi or Kamuzu, darling?" Sinclair dodged the tin of baby powder. They both gazed down at their little miracle.

"Sinclair, who on earth are we going to ask to look after Vicky when we go to the celebrations tomorrow, we really can't take her around with us, but I would like to go. So many international celebrities are coming." Sinclair gave Cynthia a hug. "Don't worry old dear, all organised. Mabel said she would love to have her for the day."

The independent state of Malawi was born on 6 July 1964 and was given full member status of the British Commonwealth.

CHAPTER TWENTY THREE
UNDER A NEW FLAG

The day of Independence dawned sunny and warm and as Cynthia and Sinclair walked up towards the Secretariat, she thought that the women lining the road in their brightly coloured dresses looked for-all-the-world like enormous banks of flowers. No other Europeans were evident out on the streets but the Browns were determined to capture this moment in history on their ciné-camera.

"Pity about the printed face of President Banda covering bust and bum, somehow seems a bit irreverent but no doubt of the President's mutual admiration society's enthusiasm! Look at those women mobbing his lovely new Mercedes," said Sinclair with a grin.

However, the hood of the car had been folded down and the President's flywhisk swept from side to side briefly touching the heads of the ululating women. "Rather like the Archbishop giving a blessing at Easter," giggled Cynthia. "Oh look Sinclair," Cynthia pointed at a familiar face smiling out of a discreet black car. "There's Prince Philip." They gave him a rousing cheer and the locals surrounding them joined in. The noise was tremendous. At that moment the cars ground to a halt, obviously the crowds round the Secretariat building had mobbed the President. Cynthia and Sinclair found themselves almost nose to nose with the Prince. "Welcome to Malawi, Your Highness," Sinclair said, as Cynthia dropped a curtsey.

"Are you the only two Europeans left in the country?" Prince Philip gave a laugh and a wave as the car moved forward.

"Gosh Sinclair and to think that the nearest I've ever been to a Royal is from the gates of Buckingham Palace. They are usually so far away they look like a postage stamp. Look Sinclair, there's another familiar face." Cynthia clutched Sinclair's arm and pointed at a massive limousine bedecked with the Stars and Stripes. "Heavens above, I'm sure that's old Soapy." The car stopped abruptly beside them, a window rolled down and a large hand shot out. "Good day to you youngsters, I'm Mennen Williams, tell me about yourselves, what do you do in Malawi?"

Oblivious to the halting of the procession, the American politician and the young couple chatted and promised to meet up again during the celebrations. "I always like to get information at grassroots level. See you later perhaps?" He waved a farewell. Sinclair and Cynthia waved back until the car disappeared around a bend. "I suppose he knows he's called Soapy but do you know why Cynthia?" she shook her head. Sinclair continued "It's because he soft-soaps people". "Well I think it's rather nice that a VIP could take the time to talk to us, even if it was only soft-soaping." Cynthia pulled impatiently at Sinclair's arm. "Come on Sinclair, I've got to get back and change for the do at Government House."

"I'm still wondering why they asked us, we are rather junior you know. Could they have made a mistake?" Sinclair looked doubtful.

"Don't be silly Sinclair, the British Colonial Civil Service never makes a mistake. They look at your background you see. We've been chosen to represent the average junior Civil Service family. We have a daughter and hopefully we will have a son one day, absolutely right from the census point of view," Cynthia turned and looked straight at Sinclair. Sometimes he gave the impression of not understanding the system. It's so obvious, she thought to herself.

Two hours later they were lining up to be formally introduced by the Governor to the international guests. Only a flicker of his eyes portrayed His Excellency's astonishment when both Prince Philip and Mr. Williams appeared to know the Browns. 'Perhaps there's more to these Browns than I know, must remember to ask Giles to do a bit of a dig.'

The grounds of Government House were filled with colour, music and people. "Not so many flowered hats, tea frocks and strings of pearls as usual," whispered Cynthia wickedly. "Just look at the way His Royal Highness is eying that row of mums sitting under that tree breast feeding their babies. Bet he is making one of his comments."

Speeches were made, cameras clicked, glasses clinked and laughter tinkled across the green lawns and beautiful beds of flowers. It was a day to remember and Cynthia and Sinclair stored up as many memories as possible. "We are so lucky to be here today," Sinclair gave Cynthia a hug.

"You're right Sinclair, it's the sort of occasion we'll boast about when we're being pushed in wheelchairs along the front in Bognor Regis," Cynthia laughed, "But do you think that anyone will believe us? This whole country is unreal, our life is unreal, we're unreal too I think." There was a moment's silence. "Now don't get emotional on me Cynthia, I know you're real and here's a pinch to prove it." They both laughed, but somehow it was a moment of sadness. "Nothing will ever be quite the same from now on," said Cynthia.

The warm day drifted into a golden sunset and soon guests were taking their leave. One of the men in Prince Philip's delegation was heard to say 'it's difficult to remember which country I'm visiting these days. The old Union Jack comes down and everybody cheers madly. Then up goes a brightly coloured new flag and everyone cheers madly again. Seems no point, sad really'. 'Yes,' thought Sinclair 'bloody sad.' The young couple made their way back down to their car at the bottom of the hill. They were silent. ' Cynthia's right, nothing will ever be the same again.' Sinclair thought to himself.

Two years later, Jonathan was born under the same circumstances as Victoria. "Trust Cynthia to make the media again", they said at Zomba Club but everyone was pleased to hear of the Browns' new baby. In the excitement of the occasion, Sinclair and Cynthia overlooked that Jonathan's birth coincided with the installation of Dr Hastings Kamuzu Banda as President of Malawi, now a Republic and One-Party State, on the 6th July 1966. They certainly did not take much notice that a new Constitution was being put in place later that month when President Banda was appointed as Commander in Chief of the Armed Services with ominous widespread powers.

Back at the office, Sinclair was surprised at the number of colleagues who came to see him after the news of Jonathan's birth spread through the community. "Your wife never does things by halves", the PS boomed at Sinclair. "Right Sir, but the worry has been worth it". Sinclair took another sip of the awful office tea. Nothing mattered. Life was good.

Dr Hastings Kamuzu Banda was officially named President of Malawi. The country had been declared a republic and one-party state on 6 July 1966.

CHAPTER TWENTY FOUR
CYNTHIA GOES TO PRISON

It was 1968. Hastings Kamuzu Banda was fully and firmly established as President of Malawi, now a republic and one-party state. The British Civil Servants were beginning to sit up and take notice. Ominous changes lay ahead.

In the lovely old house just behind the back entrance of Government House, the Brown children were having their afternoon nap. Cynthia was running up a dress for Victoria when she heard a car drive in through the gate. ' Heavens,' she thought 'I hope whoever it is won't wake the children.' But when she looked out she saw it was her friend Anita Barnes who lived just up the road and had children of a similar age to Victoria and Jon.

"Sneaking away for a quick cup of tea?" Cynthia whispered through the window. "Are yours sleeping too?" "Yes and yes," Anita replied. "Thank you very much. I need to talk." She was a brisk efficient girl belonging to all sorts of different activity groups around the town. Cynthia remembered she actually ran a Keep Fit Class for a couple of years until she overdid it and had a bit of a collapse. The notice at the Club KEEP FIT CLASSES DAILY covered with a banner strip

CLOSED DUE TO ILL-HEALTH gave members a bit of a giggle. But she was a good kind friend and always ready to help those in trouble. The two women settled down on the veranda with a pot of tea and Anita explained the real reason for her visit.

"Cynthia, I know you've had some experience with grassroots teaching and I wonder whether you would consider taking a weekly class at the women's section of the Zomba Prison. Basic skills you know, reading, writing and sums, perhaps needlework too? It's voluntary work of course. The Super asked me to find someone last night at dinner and I told him I knew the very person. Says he knows you from the Theatre Club."

Anita beamed expectantly at Cynthia who looked doubtful. "I'll have to talk to Sinclair first but let me see where I have to go and what sort of women I'll have to deal with." Surprisingly, Sinclair was all for the project. " It will take you out of the house and get you back in the swing of things darling, but take precautions on security and health. Don't want you or the children catching something nasty."

The very next day, Cynthia drove over to the Prison. She rang a bell that echoed through the entire building. Feeling strangely nervous, particularly as the very sour-faced Prison Warder did not bother to reply to her cheerful 'Good morning', she meekly followed him through the massive doors reminiscent of the Tower of London. 'Good lord, that key must be 18 inches long' she thought. She felt a moment of panic as the door slammed shut behind her. Take a few deep breaths, she said to herself. Only way to fight claustrophobia!

The Prison warder led her through long dark narrow corridors to meet up with the Superintendent Alan Reed, nicknamed Broken by his pals. He turned out to be a charming man and over a big mug of tea, briefed Cynthia on the women and their needs. It seemed fairly simple, but when he took her to the Women's Compound again through endless corridors and a number of locked doors, she was horrified when they reached the Prison yard. "Dear God," she whispered, "I had no idea there would be babies as well as youngsters."

Cynthia looked at the group of women huddled outside tiny windowless rooms. They were all dressed in coarse prison dresses of an undetermined colour. The large open area surrounded by a massive wall was utterly devoid of anything to relieve the eye or entertain the mind. It was stinking hot and not a blade of grass was growing in the bleak soil. There was no colour, no comfort and an overwhelming feeling of hopelessness.

"Do you think you can do something for them?" the Super asked. "I think I can but how much freedom have I got," gulped Cynthia looking at the children playing apathetically with small stones. "Well as long as you don't let them out the door." The Super gave a wry laugh. "Some of them are political prisoners; a couple of them are quite well educated but bored, others are in for theft, that old lady over there is a murderess. She killed a baby and ate it. She was trying to restore her youth apparently. Horrid eh!"

"You keep them all mixed up in one compound? How awful." Cynthia gasped. "What's their daily routine and when can I come?" "Well" said Broken thoughtfully "I don't want this info to be spread around, in fact I don't want you to talk at all about the project Cynthia because the facilities are not really what we want, particularly for the kids. You see they're locked up in their rooms at 6pm and let out again at 6am and then they spend the day sitting out here in the open doing nothing. We're not allowed to put them to work like we do the male prisoners. I wish I could change the system but I can't at present. It's a tricky political situation."

"What happens if one of the children falls sick at night?" asked Cynthia looking at the toddlers and remembering her broken nights with unidentified fevers and teething. "Afraid they have to wait until morning," said Broken regretfully. It was the sad little faces of the children that finally persuaded Cynthia to help. "When can I start?" she asked.

It was surprisingly easy to get things organised. Firstly she borrowed a battery operated radio and cassette player. Then she gathered toys, pencils and paper and sweets. 'Those poor little kids must have something to look forward to.' Next she went over to David Whitehead's cloth factory in Blantyre. "Can you spare material scraps? I want to teach some disadvantage women how to sew and make rag mats." Cynthia came away with a big sack including pins, needles, cotton-thread and knitting wool. She was ready for action.

Soon the classes were in progress and after Cynthia got over her initial fear of being let into the compound and then locked in with the women, she began to enjoy the work more and more.

She usually commenced each session by getting the adults and children to do a sort of Keep Fit dance to the music of her small cassette player. Their sense of rhythm was amazing. The dour prison officer in charge of the women was not happy about this. "Prisoners are not suppose to enjoy anything," he growled looking over at the laughing women and dancing children.

"What about the children," she answered fiercely. "They've done nothing to deserve this kind of life." "They must suffer with their mothers," was the cryptic reply. Suffer they did, for although they were fed daily with plain rations of mealie meal and vegetables, three of the children went down with malaria and were taken to the bottom hospital. They returned several days later, emaciated and silent. "How can you keep your children in prison with you my friends. This is no life for them. You all know it isn't. Why can't you send them back to relatives in your villages?" Cynthia eyes flashed with anger as she stood in front of the reunited mothers and children.

The mothers looked at her. They really liked Cynthia and were glad she came each week. They looked forward to her visits so much. But how could she understand the hopelessness of sending their children back to the village. Who has money to spare to feed someone else's children! They kept silent but thought to themselves,' Better to have the children die of sickness here with us than die of starvation in freedom.'

Cynthia couldn't understand their attitude but she soldiered on teaching the children and adult illiterates how to read and write. While the children practiced writing, she taught the mums how to make simple clothes by hand for the children. At the end of the lessons when Cynthia gave the children some sweets, the older women knitted jumpers to the sound of traditional music, illegally played on Cynthia's tape recorder. One of the women, Prissy, warned Cynthia. "Be careful Madam, the warder is always complaining about you and your music to Mr Reed". But Cynthia smiled and put her finger to her lips, "Don't worry Prissy, I bring Mr Reed special biscuits for his tea". "Ah, Madam, you are getting to know our ways!" Prissy threw her apron over her head and laughed and laughed and everyone joined in, until the warder appeared and said sternly, "It is time for you to go Mrs Brown!"

There was much sharing of knowledge with the women teaching Cynthia traditional games whilst she taught the children English games remembered from nursery days. She showed the women how to make rag mats out of sacking and scraps of material and gave them friendship and hope on a weekly basis. It was a rewarding experience for both teacher and pupils.

About six months after the classes commenced Anita Barnes called in to see Cynthia again. She looked uncomfortable. "I gather you are doing a great job at the Prison, sorry I haven't been round before, but you know, busy, busy and the phone always ringing."

Cynthia had wondered why no enquiries had been made, but thought that the Prison had merely used Anita as a go-between. Frankly she was enjoying the work so much, she had been rather glad that there was no interference from Anita who was known as a bit of a bossy boots.

"I really love the work Anita and even though the project is supposed to be under cover, I am getting quite a bit of support from local people; clothing, material, books and sweets for the kiddies." There was a moment's silence as she poured the tea and then Anita sounding strangely uncomfortable said, "I say Cynthia I've got a favour to ask of you."

She perched on the edge of the table as Cynthia machined buttonholes on the last item of clothing for the prison children. "Carry on talking Anita, I must finish these Christmas presents for the Prison kiddies. I'm so thrilled. David Whitehead has sent sweets and the Patels have given me fruit. People are so kind." Cynthia nipped the last piece of thread off with her teeth and looked up at Anita. "I say, you do look rather miserable Anita, what's wrong?"

"Well the local Red Cross Society of Nyasaland has been caught on the hop Cynthia. The Secretary General of the International Red Cross is on a lightning tour of Africa and he's very keen on grassroots projects. He is coming to see what we are doing here and the honest truth of the matter is that apart from running First Aid courses, selling flags and running some support services like libraries at the hospitals, we're not doing much at all at village level."

She cleared her throat rather noisily and continued. "So...the National Committee of the Red Cross Society of Nyasaland has asked me to contact you and invite you to become a member of the Society so that we can bring His Nibs to see your project at the Prison." Anita looked highly embarrassed.

Cynthia was stunned. "I can't believe it Anita. I thought no one was supposed to know about the project. Somehow now I've got the feeling I've been set up. Was I really a good choice or did nobody else want to do the job, particularly a member of the Red Cross!"

Cynthia thought carefully. 'It would never do to lose my temper,' she thought. 'I cannot do anything to deny the women and children contact with such an influential personage. Someone who could even open doors and bring freedom to the children perhaps!'

Cynthia could hardly bring herself to look at Anita as she continued. "OK Anita, I'll join, but if I'm going to be used as a Red Cross project leader, then I want to speak directly to the Secretary General and tell him what the women and children need. OK? I don't want any of those old biddies interfering in the discussions because they are entirely ignorant of the project."

Anita nodded her head in agreement. There was little she could say on the matter without downgrading the National Committee. She hoped that the incident would not spoil her friendship with Cynthia, but somehow she knew it would.

The visit took place the following week and it went well. The Secretary General sat on the small veranda in the Prison Compound and talked and laughed with Cynthia as the women and children put on a little show of traditional dancing and paraded their Christmas clothes. The Committee dressed in their best frocks and hats stood in a group away from the prisoners. They looked highly uncomfortable.

Cynthia glanced over at them. 'I expect they are wondering where are the egg sandwiches and deck chairs, ah well.' She got up and went over to the group. "Come and sit down ladies. The mums and children have spread out their rag mats for you". Cynthia saw a look of horror pass between the three women as the Chairlady answered hastily. “Thank you my dear, but no thank you, I think we had better leave now as we have to organise the Reception with the Governor. Could you drop the Secretary General at my place?”

The music played on after the big door had banged shut. “Keep up the good work my dear,” the Secretary General leaned over and took Cynthia hand and patted it gently. He was a wise old man and he saw quite clearly the wide gap between the prisoners and children and the departing committee.

“Blessed are those who care, Mrs Brown. I understand and I know what needs to be done here. You and I will be in touch regularly from now on. We will make things happen. You and I will bring about change.” Much to the amusement of the women he kissed Cynthia on both cheeks as he left the compound. “Well done my dear, well done,” he murmured quietly.

“No more laughter, no more music, into your cells women, it is past 6 o’clock.” The guard drove the women and children towards the cell doors opening into blackness but as Cynthia and the Secretary General walked towards the car they stopped and listened. Muffled singing was floating through the still evening air. ‘We will overcome, we will overcome,’ “and you and I will help them Mrs Brown,” said the SG firmly as he and Cynthia drove away. “This is one project I will not forget.”

In 1971 Hastings Kamuzu Banda was voted President-for-life.

CHAPTER TWENTY FIVE
THE GYMKHANA SHOW

Sinclair blinked his eyes sleepily and untangled himself from the mosquito net. “Tea has arrived, old girl.” He leaned over and shook Cynthia awake. “Today’s the great day and I bet you a pink gin that my tomatoes are going to get me a First.” He rubbed his hands in anticipation of receiving the highly sought-after certificate from the Hon. Irene Ponsonby, H.E.’s sister, who was on a visit from Cheltenham.

Sinclair called out to Victoria and Jonathan and eventually they wandered in from their bedrooms and sprawled on the bed beside him. What gorgeous children he thought to himself and how the years have flown.

“Did you finish your painting in time?" He asked Cynthia as she rose up from her side of the bed and padded over to the easel in the corner of her bedroom. “What do you think of it?” she asked. Sinclair gazed at the brightly coloured canvas. There was nothing very recognisable. “What have you called it?” he asked cautiously. “Well I was thinking of Sunrise over the Palombe Plains.” Cynthia replied rather uncertainly. Sinclair looked more closely at the painting. “Good Lord Cynthia, the picture’s full of funny little hills.

How can you say it's a picture of a plain"? Cynthia looked rather uncertain as she replied. "Well it's symbolic Sinclair, you know what I mean and it shows all the insurmountable problems facing the villagers, locusts, leprosy and so on............"

"What about the Taiwanese," asked Sinclair grimly! They both thought about the incredible vegetable project they had visited last month. Row after row of military-precise upstanding vegetables, all the same height. Not a weed in sight and all the plants fed by night soil collected in foul-smelling buckets. As Sinclair said when he returned home, "It's put me off carrots for life." "Perhaps I should have put the Taiwanese in the painting somehow," giggled Cynthia. "I know you don't understand my kind of art Sinclair so just shut up and celebrate when I get a certificate."

"Come on kids let's celebrate now," Sinclair swept up Jon and with Victoria running and jumping behind he did a wild dance around the room singing as he went. "With your hands you clap, clap, clap, with your feet you tap, tap, tap"... Cynthia threw pillows at him until he collapsed on the bed. She fell on the bed beside him and they all four went into a big bear hug. Sinclair nuzzled her neck. "I do love you very much darling even if I can't understand one inch of any of your paintings."

"It's your public school education what's done it." Laughed Cynthia. "You can't spell, your history and geography are highly suspect, but come to think of it, you do behave rather well..." They continued to lie in a happy family huddle until Cynthia said briskly.

"Now come on all of you, let's get moving. Don't want to be late. We'll take Emma and the children with us for the morning Sinclair, The children can play in the playground and after lunch, they can have a sleep under that big jacaranda. I'll take a blanket."

After breakfast Sinclair polished his Show vegetable entry, six beautifully formed tomatoes and, when they arrived at the Club just before 11am, they were greeted by a large group of already well-oiled friends who were not in the least bit interested in the show, just glad to have found a different excuse for a party.

"Put that old rubbish down somewhere you two and let's get down to some serious drinking." Jacko said as he made a place for them both and bawled for service. Soon the meagre show offerings were forgotten and the real reason for meeting up was confirmed. A good thrash was in the making. "What did you think of the Queen's Birthday Parade yesterday Cynthia? Your first one, n'est pas? Jacko gave Cynthia a friendly nudge with his elbow.

"Yes I've missed the previous ones, you know babes and long leave, but Sinclair had told me about the rather moving and ancient ceremony. But I wasn't prepared for yesterday's incredible white uniforms covered with green damp patches and medals and I couldn't believe that those plumed helmets were still worn." "The PS was absolutely stuffed into his outfit. His face was purple and then when they all raised their swords and called out, 'Three cheers for Her Majesty the Queen rah! rah! rah!,' I nearly died laughing."

"Laughing," said Jacko in astonishment. "Laughing at the finest service in the world, you want to have a word with your wife Sinclair." Jacko turned away in an obvious huff but Cynthia continued to laugh and carry on with the story.

"...then old Major Harrison rode his horse up the veranda steps to the Bar and he stayed there for three hours downing gins while his horse ate the peanuts. Didn't you tell me some other old codger did that once Sinclair? Anyway what was odd, none of the other drinkers seemed to notice, except to say 'cheers' occasionally?" One of the older men in the party, Major Lancelot Franklin, looked at Cynthia in amazement. "What's strange about that young lady? Old Harrison's been doing that for years, part of the Zomba Queen

Birthday Parade celebrations now." Cynthia stopped laughing. She realised that they were all quite serious and saw nothing wrong in the extraordinary events of yesterday. 'I wonder if I'll end up as nutty as the rest of them,' she thought.

Ceremonial Parade

on the occasion of the

Official Birthday

of

Her Majesty Queen Elizabeth II

held at

Zomba

at 10.00 a.m.

Saturday, 8th June, 1963

Queen's Birthday Parade: Programme- several years previous.

The rather tense situation was defused by a gathering noise at the front door of the Club. Suddenly the double doors burst open and to everyone's surprise in walked the Taiwanese delegation. The first two men carried between them an enormous lettuce about three foot in diameter, followed by a little man bearing a dinner plate on which rested a tomato as big as a football. Three men carrying a massive marrow between them brought up the tail end of the delegation and there was a respectful silence as they passed into the exhibition hall. Then pandemonium broke out.

Jacko laughed so much that he fell backwards and broke a glass and a chair. There was a rush to the Bar and doubles were ordered all round. It seemed that everyone was determined to get drunk in the quickest possible time and when the awards were made the bar was full to overflowing. Sadly, the exhibition hall was quite empty apart from the Hon. Irene Fitzpatrick, who gave a fairly long and entirely unsuitable speech, after which she presented, with great ceremony, all the Best Vegetables certificates to six bewildered and non-comprehending Taiwanese sitting in the front row. "Such a bloody shame really," said Jacko as he peered in at the ceremony.

Later that night Sinclair and Cynthia made their way home. "Enjoy yourself darling?" he asked sleepily. "Lovely, and by the way I got a FIRST for my painting, so that's you shot down in flames," said Cynthia "But why were they so touchy about the Queen's Birthday Parade. I thought it was enormously funny?" "Never laugh at the Queen, never laugh at the Colonial Civil Service and never laugh at Zomba rituals. Just isn't done old girl. The Colonial Civil Service is a dying band of very special and dedicated people. The last of the bloody white ants, in fact." Sinclair collapsed on her shoulder and as she drove home Cynthia thought to herself. "They're a very sensitive lot. Wonder what Sinclair meant about white ants, I must ask him."

She opened the door of their newly acquired Blackwood Box and tiptoed into the bedroom where dear Emma was babysitting.

“Children been good Emma"? Cynthia asked. There was a crash behind her as Sinclair fell over the rocking horse. She helped him to the bed where he lay there groaning. “I tell you what Cynthia old girl, I wonder if those Taiwanese understand that although they may have walked off with all the vegetable prizes they’ll never beat the Colonials. They’re foreigners you see”.

Cynthia sat down at the dressing table to take off her make-up. She thought about Sinclair’s words. “Heaven help me, he’s becoming as nutty as the rest of them” but as she got into bed and planted a kiss on his cheek ‘Nutty they are but there’s definitely something special about them all”.

Sinclair opened one eye. “By the way Cyn, I’ve got a transfer. Field Station, tell you more in the morning...” ‘Good for Sinclair, not so good for me’ thought Cynthia, ‘but I did say for better or worse and who knows it might be fun!’

Down through the years it became increasingly clear that Banda was totally in control of the country and its people. He assumed a God-like role synonymous with the concept of the country itself, running some government ministries; the political machine; the ruling party and the economy.

CHAPTER TWENTY SIX
TEN YEARS ON

Sinclair sat at his desk and stared out at the dry golden bush. It was his fifth year at the small Agricultural Station of Mkonde, near Mzuzu, his tenth year of sweltering October heat, his tenth year of ploughing through the mud in the rainy season, and he had loved every minute of it. Admittedly his way of life had changed somewhat since Victoria and Jonathan were born but Cynthia was a good old girl and had been fairly tolerant of his rather wild bachelor friends. She even organised a regular gambling evening with the boys, laying on a fantastic meal for them before going off to the Mzuzu Club to play squash with Kikki'.

'Poor old Kikki, funny how people always said that,' he thought, 'Damn good sport though, never mentioned a word about the fun and games up at the Lake when Cynthia went overseas for her brother's wedding. Everyone thought she was after Jacko, but then she went and married a black preacher from Mzuzu and went over to America to help him run a parish in North Carolina.'

He pondered 'How on earth am I going to take life back in Zomba'. He glanced down at the official communication he had just received. The document was brutally simple. 'In order to facilitate smooth staff handover and accelerate the Africanisation programme, it has been decided to withdraw all overseas staff from out-stations; henceforth these officers will act as Regional Field Officers attached to Headquarters in Zomba and will be responsible for the smooth hand-over to a Malawian successor and the joint implementation of training programmes in present areas of operation'.

Sinclair thought about his life at the bush station, his easy relationship with his staff and rather detached association with authority and decided, with a careful wipe of his perspiring head, that this was definitely not a change for the good. 'I really don't like the way things are going or the way Banda is going, maybe it is better to be out in the sticks'. He leaned back on his chair and enjoyed the silence. But it was too silent.

"Yassein," he shouted. "Bring tea." There was no reply, so swinging his legs to the floor; he marched to the door leading to the back kitchen, flung it open and roared again "Yassein" A guilty figure rose up from a crouch by the hissing fire, hastily thrusting a book into his apron pocket. "What the devil are you doing, Yassein? Come on; bring my tea, its ten minutes late already. What are you doing anyway?"

Sinclair advanced on his cook splendidly arrayed in white kanza and red fez. "I am learning to read Bwana. The new D.C. Mr. Socrates Chilwa told us all must read so that we can take the European's job but eee Bwana, I am an old man and this reading is too much troubles. These picannins Janeti and Joni are too strange. I think Bwana this Independence is also too much trouble."

"They tell me I have Independence and then ask for more tax money. When I did not have this Independence, I was not asked for money, I footed it to this village and that village - without this Party Card. I did not have to go to big meetings if I did not want to go. I planted my maize, brewed my beer and got a little drunk but nobody told me what to do. Is there something about this Independence that I do not know? Bwana when is this Independence going to stop?"

Sinclair gazed at the old man who had looked after him ever since he came to Mkonde, teaching him the language, suffering his hangovers and once helping Cynthia to nurse him through a bad bout of malaria. "Look here Yassein you old rogue, you can't expect the Europeans to stay here for ever. You've got some good blokes at the top, be a bit tough at first though." They gazed at each other in silence. "Now come along there's a good chap and bring me my tea." Sinclair felt sorry for the old man.

"Chabwino, chabwino, Bwana." the old man said sadly, "But my heart is heavy with trouble and my head is round with all the things they are telling me. Why must all life change?" He strode off with a dignified swish of his robes, back into the security of his dark kitchen, where in a temperature of 120 degree he crouched once more and watched the kettle start to hiss and dance. "Poor old chap," thought Sinclair "He's just as fed up as I am."

The telephone jangled and Sinclair picked it up, wondering idly what he was going to do this weekend, particularly as Cynthia was Christmas shopping in Lilongwe. Yes, he must organise something.

"Hello you old bastard," a familiar voice shouted down the phone. "What are you doing this week-end? Heard you were on your own and thought you might like to drop over. Frank, Willy, Roger and Jacko and one or two of the Police chaps are coming over. Might have a game of bok-bok and a glass or two."

"Splendid Johnnie old chap, I'll be over Saturday lunchtime, should be able to find an excuse to visit your district. How's the locust situation. Can you find one or two for me to report on?" Sinclair's face broke into a smile as he talked to Johnnie Latimer Broughton. 'Good old sport was Johnnie. Heavens they'd had some good times together. Would he ever forget that Agricultural Seminar at Lilongwe Hotel. That was a party to end all parties with the Executive Officer and the Senior Accountant from the local Bank doing a tap dance on the dining room table; Jacko giving his famous Tarzan act swinging from chandelier to chandelier and that old bugger Lushington punching in all the veranda windows - only had to have ten stitches too. Party went on for two days. Good old Johnnie, Damn good sport'.

'Shame about his divorce but he would keep on visiting the mahouris down at Zomba Inn and then gave his wife Isabella a dose of the clap. Kept trying to change did old Johnnie but Bella eventually called it a day and went back to the UK. Ah well'.

Whistling the latest Party Rally song Sinclair went off to pack his bag and prepare the ground for an official visit to the remote Agricultural Station some fifty miles outside Muzuzu.

CHAPTER TWENTY SEVEN
WHITE ANTS IN THE CHIMNEY

Under the fierce mid-day sun the game of bok-bok was well under way and to the group of watching locals it seemed as if the bwanas were intent on, not only killing themselves and each other, but also on knocking down the walls of Bwana Brougton's house. Eeeeeeee! Europeans are most strange!

The last man, Danny Hogan, prepared to take his run, a fanatic on the rugby field, he was at least six foot four inches tall and weighed two hundred pounds of solid bone and muscle. He was the *piece de resistance* of the challenging team.

He landed at the top of the line crashing heavily onto the groaning undulating snake of backs. The line wavered, broke and collapsed and when both teams had staggered to their feet, Cecil Lucas was clutching his wrist and Danny Hogan lay motionless. "Think I've broken my wrist chaps." murmured Cecil apologetically. "Don't think you can get out of making a back for our team." shouted Roger. "I say what's up with our Dan?" They all moved over and gazed down at the silent figure, Sinclair bent down and felt his pulse. "Alive but out cold. Looks as if it might be concussion. Let's put him on the couch on the veranda. Must finish the game." They laid him reverently on the couch, placed a bottle of whisky beside him and went back to the game but somehow it didn't seem such fun anymore.

"I know, how about a game of Dare," Jacko suggested. "That's it, I'm on." chorused several voices. Sinclair looked dubious. He remembered some of the previous dares and the rather embarrassing consequences.

"Come on chaps, got to do something, can't sit here with a bottle and go bush happy," roared Jacko. They sat down under a wild fig tree and after a few rounds of beers, Dare seemed to be the idea of the year. Dividing into two teams and facing their opponents, they commenced.

"Jacko I dare you to down a full glass of whisky without taking a breath," said Sinclair. "That's not a dare old chap, that's a pleasure." He raised the brimming glass to his lips, took a deep breath and then tipped the glass. They waited for him to keel over but he didn't bat an eyelid. There was a respectful pause. "Real old colonial is Jack."

"Sinclair I double dare you to climb up the inside of Johnny's chimney." They all went inside the house taking turns to look up the small hole. "Seems a bit small," Sinclair turned to Jacko appealingly. "Take your clothes off man. Where's your initiative?" roared Jacko. Roughly debagged by willing helpers, starkers, Sinclair was pushed into the fireplace and on up the chimney as far as they could reach, muffled yells and lumps of old soot falling back into the room.

Jacko and Roger ran outside and scaled the walls onto the roof where they stood by the chimneystack shouting encouragement down to Sinclair, at the same time passing the whisky bottle to each other. As Jacko lowered the bottle for the second time he spotted a cloud of dust on the road leading into the Station "Hey boys someone's coming." The vehicle came into view. "My God it's the P.S. Quick lads throw up a piece of hosepipe." Leaning down over the inside of the chimney he called down to Sinclair.

“Hey Sinclair old boy, bit of an emergency. The PS is just about to arrive. Try not to yell there’s a good chap. Suck on this hosepipe for a spot of air and we’ll get you out as soon as we can.” He fed the pipe into Sinclair’s gaping mouth and shouted to the other men below. “Quick boys, there’s not a moment to lose.”

And so it was when the Permanent Secretary walked up the veranda steps he saw a group of his young men delicately mopping the brow of Danny Hogan, “Touch of malaria Sir.” while another group equally solicitous were bandaging Cecil’s wrist. “Fell off his pencil, Sir.” and the room having been hastily deodorised with Jayes Fluid and smelling like a British Railway cloakroom, rocked with scarcely concealed laughter.

“Good chaps, my dear boys, how nice to see you all relaxing.” The PS peered round fondly through his National Health spectacles. “I say room’s a bit of a mess what?” He gazed at the pools of Jayes Fluid, the overturned furniture and the large lumps of soot round the fireplace. In a flash Jacko stood with his back to the mantelpiece, his head framed by a large print of Her Majesty the Queen, which was under heavy white ant attack.

“Just having a bit of a spring-clean Sir,” he said brightly “Must keep it home from home”. “Quite so, my boy must keep up the standards.” The PS said uncertainly. “And keep the flag flying Sir,” Jacko added.

Up in the chimney Sinclair wondered if this was death. He could hardly breathe and he knew that movement was impossible until the PS decided to leave. What an inglorious end he though but perhaps a shade better than being recalled to the UK. He decided a short nap was the only answer to his immediate problem and that’s how they found him three hours later after the PS had been cheered on his way. One by one the other men went off to their lonely stations dotted around the area.

Later that evening after a wash, change of clothes and several strong drinks Johnnie, Jacko and Sinclair sat down to goat stew peppered with fried black ants. "Delicious Johnnie old boy," said Sinclair settling back in his chair. "Wish my old Yassein could cook goat like this," Johnnie took a long pull at his drink.

"It's our ants my boy, they really are the best in the territory. My cookie catches them with sugar water, fries them to perfection in a dry pan and then rubs them to powder between two stones. Best ant pepper in Africa. I'm seriously thinking of exporting to Europe." They burst out laughing at the thought of selling ants at grocers in the UK and Jacko gave a demonstration on how he would approach various stores in London.

"Just imagine trying to sell them to Harrods Food Hall," said Sinclair. " But seriously my friends do you think we'll ever fit in overseas again. Who would understand our life out here? The trouble is there's nowhere else to go. We're a dying breed, the old Colonial Civil Servant, Florence Nightingale of the bush, miniature Cecil Rhodes on a shoe-string, doomed to retire to a semi-detached in Brighton."

Jacko looked at Sinclair in astonishment. "I say old chap that's a bit thick, getting sentimental and all that. Who says we are on our way out?" Sinclair gazed into his glass and raised it towards Jacko and Johnnie. To his alarm he felt tears coming. "Lads, I give you a toast to those indomitable white clothed workers who are on the point of total extermination. I give you that happy brave intoxicated breed - the white ants of Africa."

CHAPTER TWENTY EIGHT
THE WINDS OF CHANGE

Sinclair's bachelor friend Cecil William Jones was already on his second lunch- time pink gin when Sinclair walked into the Club.

"How about a game of golf on Saturday old lad, 'bout time you had a bit of exercise." Sinclair ignored the reference to his thickening waistline. "Who are you playing with?" he asked suspiciously. "Because if you've asked Uphill Thomas and the PS, you can count me out, I can't stand the way the bloody little creep sucks up to the PS and then pays that caddie Joyful to cheat. That damn boy can carry a ball half a mile between his toes."

"Oh come on now, old boy, we all know about Upfill but he's the only 16 handicap I can beat and there's an element of roulette about the game. Anyway it's only a few bob." Cecil peered round the club to check if Uphill or the PS were in hearing distance. "Beware listening ears, Sinclair," he muttered.

"You're not getting the point Cecil," said Sinclair stubbornly. "These new contract blokes are all the same. All bloody nits with suburban minds. Not a bit interested in the country or the people. Come here with one thing in mind, collecting their twenty-five percent gratuity and paying off the mortgage on their semi-detached in Cheam or West Wickham, always knocking the colonials and fawning round the bloody foreign visitors."

He took a vigorous swig of his beer and glared round to see if any of the offenders were near. "Look," he said bitterly, "They don't even come to the Club until six because their wives tell them it's not nice." "Oh be reasonable old chap, we don't have to like them, just get along with them", said Cecil soothingly. "Must keep up the flag, esprit de corps and all that."

"Cheers," he added loudly as an after-thought. All round the wide bar counter glasses were raised automatically to an orchestra of "Cheers." Cecil continued. "I think some of them are quite good chaps, very sound technically, if somewhat a little unpolished."

He paused. "Did I tell you about the dinner party those new people, the Huggins, gave last week? They served some sort of cottage pie and she wore bedroom slippers, very droll." "Old Brown sherry too I suppose." Sinclair leaned back in his chair. "I'm telling you they'll be the death of this country. The poor old locals don't know where they stand."

"They invite the cook to use the family bath and sit down to breakfast with them and then when cookie takes the benefits a step further and starts feeding all his friends and family at the back door, Father Christmas turns into an SS colonel and starts weighing the sugar, marking the gin bottle and fining him ten bob off his wages."

"Ah well," said Cecil, "Don't let it get to you. Have another drink or two or three." "No can do Cecil, I've got a meeting at the office in ten minutes. Just came in to book the squash court for this evening. Jacko and I are having a workout. See you for a drink after the game!"

Sinclair went off to his office and Cecil gazed down into his vanishing gin. 'Trouble with old Sinclair he cares too much about this country. Best not to get too close - like me for instance. Keep your distance from everyone. Then you can move onto the next posting without any problems'. He drank the remaining gin and called for another. Somehow in the back of his mind he acknowledged that there was a fault in his philosophy. 'Could it be that he was wrong and that was why he was so lonely!

By the 1990s it was estimated that some 250 000 people had disappeared or had been murdered during Banda's 31-year-reign. Opposition to his totalitarian one-party rule had grown, spurred on by the end of the Cold War and the withdrawal of international aid to the Third World.

CHAPTER TWENTY NINE
SACRIFICIAL LAMBS

Back at the office Sinclair waited for the staff to drift in. God, they were bad timekeepers. He remembered the disastrous Field Day held last month on Wednesday May 10th. They had all agreed the date and wrote it down in their diaries. What happened? Some came on Wednesday 17th. 'Sir you did say a Wednesday I believe?' Others came on the 10th June, 'you did say thc 10th Sir!' and three wandered in on 30th May, 'didn't we agree May Sir?'

'They are certainly not ruled by clock and calendar', he thought to himself, 'maybe that's why they are such a relaxed and happy people...' Sinclair rubbed his stomach. 'I'm sure that I am getting an ulcer'. He lay back and closed his eyes. 'How will I ever get this office sorted out and handed over before Independence and how are we all going to cope with the planned changes of political and administrative rule. Changes that in some cases have appointed a low-grade worker with political clout to a senior position over educated and senior staff. Already there's a different atmosphere in our office. People are watchful and from what I overheard last week the locals are really getting quite militant. Wonder if there'll be violence. Heavens I feel tired. I must get that bilharzia test', he thought.

He opened his eyes and stared across the office courtyard and watched as a long line of bearers headed up by Anthony Hallerton weaved across the central courtyard. It was obviously a walking field project. The locals called it footing. Probably no vehicle was available again. Bloody transport section. Poor old Ant, never married but what a great Civil Servant. Never put a foot wrong in his entire career. Sinclair examined the line of bearers more closely. Where was the tent? He could make out a card table, a chair, boxes of beers, and even a bottle of gin and supermarket bags of what must be food.

"Going out for a couple of weeks Anthony?" he shouted. "Good heavens no old boy just for the afternoon but must be prepared." Anthony smiled. His eyes twinkled behind his thick glasses and jamming his old Scout hat on his head, he shouted, "See you this evening at the bar." Sinclair leaned back in his chair, smiled and said to himeself. 'There are not many of them left, but Anthony must be one of the original White Ants'.

Suddenly he noticed a tall black man walking towards the office. He called out. "Hallo Pythagoras, come and have a cup of coffee, fill me in on how the finance seminar went in Lilongwe." Soon the two young men who had worked together for three years were chatting over the seminar results and then out of the blue Sinclair asked. "You know Py I often wondered how you got that name. Is there a story behind it?" The handsome young black laughed. "Actually my name is Percy Nduzu but when I was at high school I was considered rather a wizard at maths and the teacher nicknamed me Pythagoras and somehow it stuck right through university. Even my wife calls me Py." They laughed. Sinclair knew that Py was one of the more privileged locals. His father was a wealthy rural businessman and they were well connected with the emerging black politicians.

There was silence for a moment. Both of them were searching for the right words to continue the conversation. Sinclair broke the ice. "Py there's a lot of gossip about the real value of Independence to the people who put the old man in the hot seat. But what worries me is that there is violence brewing between the Civil Servants and the President's Young Pioneers. Let's be quite frank Py, the Young Pioneers are very anti-white. Give me your honest opinion do you think there will be violence next week? I hear the Senior Civil Servants have had just about enough of the bullying by the gangs roving the towns and beating up innocent people on their way home from work. What do you think will happen Py?"

Py remained silent for a few minutes. Obviously again he was choosing his words with care. "Yes Sinclair I think there will be violence but you whites will be OK unless you get in the way. That could be unfortunate. There are so few white settlers in this country now, just the odd farmer and tea and coffee families and you British Civil Servants. Well you are really sort of working visitors." They both laughed and he continued.

"But I am sure there will be violence between us blacks. You see we're very tribal and there will be a lot of jostling for power and top jobs. Already there's talk of moving the capital from Zomba to Lilongwe, Banda's province ...", he paused, "...and there'll be plenty of retribution for ancient quarrels, unfulfilled promises, cheating, injuries - so yes there will be violence. You whites have just got to steer clear of it. What worries me is the breakdown in the relationship between the young and old in this country. Traditionally our youngsters would never gang up against the elders and behave in this violent way. Trouble is I think there's some imported influence at work and maybe drugs are being encouraged. I heard of some traditional healers dispensing some very powerful herbal mixtures." Py leaned back on his wicker chair and closed his eyes. "It's all very worrying Sinclair."

"So you think the Commies have sneaked into the country." Sinclair picked up the thread and countered when Py didn't answer. "OK Py so we whites must stay clear of trouble but there are a lot of ugly rumours going round the town. A plump white woman earmarked as a top prize in a raffle. There talk of cars and houses being appropriated AND all our belongings. We are all worried and a few of the ex-pats are planning to ship wives and children back to Britain pronto. Are we over-reacting?"

Again Py waited for a while before answering. "Sinclair we've been friends for quite a while now so I won't pull any punches. Yes there are some angry blacks shouting off their mouths trying to incite people to violence but look at the nature of us blacks in this country. We are a pretty even-tempered lot and have always enjoyed a sort of paternalistic relationship with you British Civil Servants. You have always treated us fairly, but never quite as equal adults of course."

Py was not smiling as he made this statement and Sinclair knew in his heart of hearts that this was a fair comment. Py continued "Of course that's where you really went wrong because you never allowed us to take a full measure of responsibility across the board until it was almost too late. Even last week, in this office I heard Peter Punter shouting at old Norton Makwecha 'Haven't you learnt anything from me in all the years I've been here', and do you know what Norton replied? He said, "I think I have not learnt because you have not always taken the time to teach me WHY I must do something, but I have always done exactly what you told me to do."

"You see the difference. A subtle weapon of power, withholding the logical reason for an action?" Py rubbed his forehead. "I'm getting a headache thinking of it again. I was so angry Sinclair." There was a brief silence until Sinclair commented.

"I don't blame you for being angry Py, Peter's so bitter. He should have gone home as soon as possible after his wife died having that last baby. He is blaming the country without realising it and taking it out on junior staff. But look how many people white and black rushed to give Pippa blood. The hospital just could not stop the bleeding."

Py replied, "Of course I understand about Peter but incidents like that are not making the change-over any easier and make no mistake we blacks are not going to have an easy time in the years ahead. Just look at what has happened in the Independent countries to the North of us. Corruption, bribery, misappropriation of aid money, so I predict the rich blacks will get richer and the poor blacks will stay poor or poorer...that's why I've applied to go back to Britain and take up further studies. With any luck I'll find a job over there and stay indefinitely."

Sinclair looked astonished. "Don't you want a piece of the action Py? Surely your father's got influence and is fairly well heeled. A good Government job would be available for you at the very least, if not a political post!"

Py looked away. "I'm not a political animal Sinclair and my father is being milked dry by hungry politicians. Money promotes power and they are taking it any way they can. My only hope is to leave the country Sinclair but I hope that if I die over there someone will send back my old bones to be laid to rest with my ancestors in Ntaja,"

There was nothing more to be said. Sinclair went over to his friend and tapped him lightly on the shoulder. "Never mind my friend, eventually all us Colonials will have to return to the UK and God knows how we will fare but let's keep in touch. Who knows, may be we could start an African Homeland on the Yorkshire Moors!"

" Sounds a bit too chilly for me," Py replied and they both laughed but the sadness lingered between them. 'It will never, never ever be the same', thought Sinclair "Goodbye Sinclair," Py shook Sinclair's hand in the traditional way. "Thank you for your friendship, I always felt you understood us blacks a little more clearly than most whites. I'll write to you as soon as I'm settled in Edinburgh again."

Sinclair watched his friend walk down towards the car park.

Little did he know then that Py would never reach the UK but would be found the following week hacked to death in the Dedza Hills. He was one of many innocent victims in a corrupt political arena. There was a grim message pinned to his mutilated body. 'Father of Percy Nduzu, unless you want to find another son dead outside your door tomorrow, stop helping Kamuzu's enemies'.

"Py's father wouldn't help Kamuzu's enemies! He's a traditionalist and really believes the old man speeches on progress and development. No, Py's murder was a put up job, someone jealous of the family's money, education and their large and successful farm", thought Sinclair bitterly as he watched Py's coffin lowered into the family's traditional burial ground. "Now it will never bloody well be the same again. Why, why did it have to happen?"

The mournful wailing of the women echoed around the Dedza hills and seemed to multiply in volume. Sinclair felt he was going to vomit and ran to his car where he wept bitter tears for his friend. No, it will never be the same again.

CHAPTER THIRTY
IF AT FIRST YOU DON'T SUCCEED

Ted sat listening to the Departmental weekly radio programme Farm News. The Jomba family were belting out the latest jingle inviting all Malawians to register as voters. It was true that the 1961 Elections were overwhelmingly successful when the use of symbols on the voting papers helped the largely illiterate rural people to mark their choice of leader. However, now it was felt that since national post-Independence education plans had been in place for some time, it might be a good idea to run a trial research programme to gauge how much improvement had been made where adult literacy was concerned.

'Must contact Sinclair and find out how those Registration trials are going'. Ted crossed the courtyard, breezed into Sinclair's office and sat down on his desk. "So what's with the registration trials?" Sinclair rescued his coffee cup and said with a grin. "Do you want the good news or the bad news?" Ted gave the thumbs up signal and Sinclair continued.

"As you know Ted, Cynthia's Bambo Jomba puppet theatres have been very successful in the various educational programmes of a number of Ministries, particularly agriculture and those catchy jingles went down well on radio too as well in the puppet shows. I really think the villagers are pleased to see the information units coming to their village with news on the benefits of independence and plenty of funny cartoons. No longer do they have to toil up to the Boma for village information!"

Sinclair took a large gulp of tea and continued. "Also you know it was a bloody good idea of the PS to suggest to the British MP who came on a fact-finding mission that it would really help national communication if each village headman could be given a radio and monthly supply of batteries. Apparently that scheme is definitely going ahead". Sinclair gave Ted a grin. "You know Permanent Secretaries do have their uses Ted," and fell off his chair as Ted threw a folder at him.

Order restored, Sinclair continued. "Well to cap it all I think the travelling puppet show is a success because it links the village people to Government development plans, it brings families together and what is more they learn and laugh together and quite simply its all about real village life and real village people."

Ted nodded his head in agreement. "Just like the British Archer Family radio series but you are quite right Sinclair and another benefit is that the educational entertainment has brought all age groups of a community together. They go away with knowledge that is of use to them all and lets face it they have fun. It's a very good concept." Sinclair grinned. "Absolutely right Ted and with the youngsters enjoying formal schooling they are able to help the semi-literate elders still struggling with adult literacy classes to understand without loss of dignity."

Ted finished his tea and banged the cup down on table. "Now come on Sinclair, stop waffling, we both know the value of this programme, now tell me what happened on the Registration campaign?"

Sinclair stood up and walked to the window. He was silent for a moment and turned to face Ted. "You know Ted, I think it was a bloody good idea of Mark Chirwa's to use the radio and information unit programme to launch the trial Registration campaign and let Bambo Jomba explain the Registration process." "I hope it was a success old lad," Ted said with a laugh. "Quite honestly more than a few of the old diehards at Head Office thought it was a potty idea."

SCHOOLCHILDREN ENJOY BAMBO JOMBA
The Ministry of Information mobile units played a very important role in the grassroots development programme after Independence.

Sinclair pulled a face and continued. "Well Koma Koma did a fine job getting the Ntaja villagers together and the Ministry of Information unit was only thirty minutes late arriving. We could hear it coming for a couple of miles back blaring out the agricultural jingles, which the crowd commenced to sing. It was quite a party. You

ought to have seen the fight for front places."
Ted said cautiously "Sounds good so far."

"Wait for it," Sinclair gave a broad grin. The driver turned on the music to maximum, opened the back door of the unit and disappeared behind the curtains. The front curtain opened with a roll of drums. You should have heard the cheers when Bambo Jomba came onto the stage and went through the questions three times using his personal details. Of course he did all the usual funny things like losing his pencil and pretending he could not find it behind his ear, much shouting and laughter of course...and when Jomba asked them if they all understood everything, the crowd with a mighty roar said, "Yes." So he invited them all to come and queue up outside the Registration tent and each fill in a form and what did we get?" Sinclair couldn't stop grinning. "We got over a hundred forms filled in with Bambo Jomba's details!" Ted nearly fell off his chair he laughed so much. "That's called being hoisted by your own petard Sinclair," as he dodged a file throw at his head. "If at first you don't succeed, try, try again old lad. It's back to the drawing board."

Order was eventually restored but after Ted left, still laughing and shaking his head, Sinclair sat back and thought about the trial results. He also thought about the lectures, the training sessions, field days, handouts, the monthly magazine and all the technical papers researched by wave after wave of highly qualified staff.

'What's it all about. Have we made any real impact at all! Is life any better here in this country for us being here! Or are we just a bunch of do-gooders trying to impose an English way of life on people who are just too polite to tell us to bugger off. They are perfectly content with what they have it seems to me. They certainly have a much more secure family life than in most countries in the world'.

He was lost in thought when Zeev Sharon, an Israeli researcher popped his head round the door. When he saw Sinclair's face, he came in and sat down. "What's up my friend?" Sinclair poured out his frustrations. "I feel I have wasted years of my life. Too many years of giving out useless information to a people who have mastered the art of primitive survival against all odds, and when do we ever listen to them?"

Zeev remained silent. He willed Sinclair to spill it all out.

"OK, so we brought our education system to them and made a great deal of fuss about right-angles and straight lines when they just don't exist in their world." Sinclair rubbed his eyes and head. His whole body seemed to hurt with frustration.

"For heavens sakes, Zeev, we marched into this country and created a map according to the map of England. You know, nicely shaped boundaries, straight down rivers and along the top of mountains. We drew neat and irreversible lines through ancient water and land rights creating chaos and war between communities too. Yes, we did some good things like establishing a health service which provides a medical programme to ensure that seven out of ten children survive their first year, but now, just when the blacks are beginning to stand up and question what we have done in this country, when we could investigate the possibility of a different kind of relationship, a partnership perhaps, we decide to pull down the flag and bugger off."

Zeev walked to the window and thought about this sensitive man, his friend. What could he say to ease the pain of Sinclair's coming and inevitable departure from Malawi. Pain made worse because of the bewilderment as to why it should have to happen.

"Sinclair, my friend, it's difficult for me as an Israeli, to see the present situation from an English perspective. We Israelis are relatively new, modern if-you-like, colonialists, so, like the Romans at the height of their power, the Portuguese, the Germans and the French in those early days of move-in and plunder, we are not benign. We are not cricket on the green and egg sandwiches with the vicar. It's 'do it our way or else'... and if we do not reach an agreement, it's jump-in-boots-and-all to make it happen."

He eased the tension with a laugh. "We also have an ancient religious background which completely justifies righteous anger supported by violence. Just read the Old Testament!"

He continued. "It seems to me that you English have a terrible burden of guilt, always trying to make up for mistakes or possible oppression. But you see there is a very real need for a strict discipline of change if you are committed to imposing it. England commenced her colonisation programme during Victoria's reign on the platform '***WE MUST BE RIGHT - WE'RE BRITISH!***' and has spent the last fifty years apologising. But I think your biggest mistake in Africa was to try and turn a Third World country into Little England. Won't work." He gave Sinclair a bear hug. "Cheer up Sinclair, we all have our days of doubt and uncertainty. Come over for supper tomorrow. We'll talk some more. To-morrow's another day."

Walking his friend to his car, Sinclair tried to keep a smile on his face,"Thanks Zeev, I don't agree with you but I've enjoyed our talk, see you soon". But as he watched the car drive off, he almost felt tears coming to his eyes and stamped his feet in rage. 'No, no, my friend, you don't understand, all the tomorrows be the last day for all of us'.

CHAPTER THIRTY ONE
BLOODY INTERNATIONAL EXPERTS

"Another bloody load of overseas experts coming today," Sinclair stirred his breakfast coffee and gazed out at the lowering clouds. "Ah well" said Cynthia brightly, "Maybe the rains will break today and that will put paid to any embarrassing rural trips." "Afraid not old dear, the PS particularly wants us to show them that new Co-operative set up down the other side of the mountain. Terrible road though, even without the rains."

Sinclair groaned and remembered last week's unfortunate incident when he was overheard calling a visiting delegation 'international parasites'. "Pull yourself together Brown," the PS had said sternly. "Can't let the side down at this delicate stage of negotiations. Malawi needs international funding and training if the country is to make a go of it. So kindly refrain from any further ill-timed remarks."

It was a fair rebuke but Sinclair knew it was going to be difficult to get through the day without blotting his copybook once more. He appealed to Cynthia who was busy getting the children ready for school. "Cyn, they're so arrogant. The last lot did a three-day tour of Africa, for heavens sake, and then went back and wrote a book called 'Africa Problems and How They Should be Resolved'. Said it was a Bestseller. Can you believe it?" Cynthia looked at Sinclair thoughtfully. "It's just as well we are finishing up here next month," she said to herself. "Otherwise, I really believe that Sinclair will crack up! Trouble is he cares too much about the place. Who is going with you Sinclair?" Cynthia put her arms round her husband. 'My heavens he's looking drawn and thin' she thought. "Oh the usual crowd. Basil, Les Thorpe, Frank and Percy Koma Koma," Sinclair replied listlessly. "Well, let them deal directly with the visitors and take a back seat yourself," said Cynthia firmly. "You've only another six weeks to go and then it's back to Britain for good. Enjoy the sun and the warmth while you can."

The delegation of five stood in a row on the steps of the Secretariat. Dressed identically in off-white safari suits and horn-rimmed glasses and carrying matching brief cases, the leader standing in the middle was immediately identified by his extra height 'Possibly the result of elevated shoes,' Sinclair thought nastily.

"Hello there," the leader called out. The flashing white teeth seemed almost obscene to Sinclair but the group seemed friendly enough and after a briefing by the PS, the men piled into three battered Land Rovers and set off up the mountain.

A picnic shared at the top of Zomba Mountain gave the visitors the opportunity to take photographs from the magnificent Queen's View. The sun danced on the distant lakes and stretched out to touch the massive Mulanje Mountains on the horizon. Small villages dotted about the plains were identified by curls of blue smoke spiralling mistily to mingle with black smoke billowing from a nearby grass fire. 'That village will have to watch it' he thought. It was a magical canvas of colour that never failed to hit Sinclair where it hurts whenever he saw it. 'God help me, I'm going to miss this place.'

However, the special moment was ruined by the harsh voice of the leader of the delegation. "Not so impressive as the views in our country, but not bad, not bad at all," Sam the leader remarked. "Take a shot for the book Stan." Stan obeyed and Basil and Thorpe seeing that Sinclair was about to explode went over and hissed. "Don't say a word Sinclair!"

MOUNTAIN FORESTS
Plantations of trees planted on both Zomba and Mlanje Mountains have opened up a lucrative timber industry.

Further developments were interrupted when suddenly a small buzzer rang. In unison the visitors checked their watches, opened their brief cases and took out some pills, which they swallowed with bottled water. "Brought safe water with us from Home,' one of the delegation remarked with a hearty laugh as he swallowed half a dozen pills. "Got to keep your bugs at bay."

"What are you taking and why?" asked Sinclair curiously. "Antibiotics, anti-histamines, daily vitamins and minerals", beamed the leader. "Can't afford to get sick on an important trip like this. Of course the pre-trip shots were a different story, rather nasty, in fact some of us were hospitalised but we are covered for cholera, smallpox and liver viruses and have special soaps to kill bacteria, fleas, lice and ticks."

"What about leprosy and scorpions," asked Sinclair nastily, "There's one climbing up your collar by the way." In the ensuing panic several bottles of the precious bottled water were spilt and the delegation spent some time searching each other for further scorpions. A rather evil-looking spider was removed from the inside of a hat, and assorted ticks from socks. An overall air of panic was developing among the visitors.

"Nasty things scorpions and spiders. Rotten bites. One of my staff eventually had to have his leg off". Basil looked sad as he munched his marmite sandwich. "My God," gasped the leader "That was a near miss. Can we carry out this survey without getting out of the vehicles?" "Heavens no," said Les. "We'll all have to get out of the vehicles and wade across the river to lighten the load otherwise the Landies will stick in the mud and we'd have a devil of a job to get them out. Could take days...but we have to tour the co-op's project on foot, have a meal with the Co-Op members of course and they've probably killed a young goat for us." The delegation looked aghast. Eat a goat!

Les continued. "Then we also have to sit and talk to party officials after the tour of the Co-op. Doubt we'll get back to Zomba before dark." The delegation looked horrified. "Maybe we should turn back," said the leader weakly. "We can't put you locals at risk." "Sorry Sir," said Les Thorpe firmly. "We have been tasked with taking you to the project and we will not let you down. Let's get back into the vehicles and go down into the valley."

The journey down the escarpment road was uncomfortable for the locals but for the visitors it was a nightmare. Sinclair noticed hands sneaking, snake-like, into briefcases with pills being swallowed dry.

'Tranquillisers shouldn't wonder, the poor buggers are frightened stiff'. He eyed them carefully. '"I wonder if any of them will crack.'

One man certainly lost his cool when a large crocodile slid into the river as they pushed the vehicles through the muddy waters. "Ran the four minute mile and then got caught up with a fish trap". Sinclair told Cynthia hours later. "I think he wet himself with fright, he was in my vehicle, definitely smelly."

Eventually the vehicles reached the village where the entire population had turned out to meet the visitors who by now were hot, soiled and completely disenchanted by the whole exercise. Protocol was maintained and everyone shook hands with everyone. It was a long process and Sinclair noticed that medical wipes were being palmed between the visitors.

Eventually large bowls of water were circulated between the visitors. "Please to wash hands before meal," whispered the little girls kneeling at the feet of the visitors. "Not feeling very hungry," gasped one of the delegation, but as Les explained firmly eat they must, otherwise the villagers would be very offended, and eat they did, even though Sinclair did catch Mac, Sam's No 2, spitting mouthfuls of food into his handkerchief.

"Just think of it as rather tough lamb, Mac," he murmured, and was taken aback by a pure unhidden look of hate. "Only trying to help," he murmured as he moved away and sat with the Chief who was an old friend and actually had a degree in Political Science.

"When are you coming up to see us in Zomba Jakob?" The Chief winked. "I'm coming up to collect wife number 6 next week, see you then." Lucy his wife, busy serving food giggled, Sinclair and her husband always enjoyed this wife joke. Wife No. 6 indeed, he could hardly afford her and the 8 children. Jakob and Lucy smiled at each other. This was turning out to be a very funny meeting indeed.

Somehow the tour of the Co-operative was carried out and in quick time too. Sinclair noticed that none of the visiting delegation made notes and all of them regularly cleaned their hands with medicated tissues. "How do you catch leprosy?" a voice tinged with anxiety asked.

"Let's get this lot back to Zomba quickly," Les Thorpe looked grim. "You know that bloody Sam put his arm round the Chief and said, "YOU are going to be my friend". "Well, you know how sensitive Jakob is when whites are patronising, so he took exception to the whole visit and told Sam, I will let you know, but I do not think I want to be your friend."

"Then the Chief told me, in Chechewa of course, to get these idiots out of his village. So let's go." Sam was most put out by their sudden departure and the journey back was slow and silent. No information was exchanged. No promises given.

However, at a meeting next day when the local officers offered to give the delegation a list of items needed to support the agricultural extension programme, Sam was quite confident and back in the driving seat. "Probably read 'How to Win Friends and Influence People all night," commented Les to Sinclair behind his hand. Sam looked up. He had heard the comment and Sinclair could see steel in his eyes. 'He's out to get back at us' he thought.

Tight-lipped Sam continued. "No need to give us a list, yesterday was quite an eye-opener by the way. However we know exactly what you need to help the agricultural extension programme and agricultural co-operatives. Leave it all in our hands Brown." Sinclair felt that there was a sting in the tail and indeed there was because months later and long after Sinclair and Cynthia had left Malawi, a large crate arrived at the Extension Aids Branch office. It was from Sam and his delegation and words stencilled on the box pronounced that it was 'A gift to fulfil the needs of Malawi'. Opened with difficulty it was found to contain a large number of assorted electric toothbrushes!

The PS, a kind-hearted man, said doubtfully that they must have got the consignments mixed up, but Basil wasn't so sure. "I'd say they were paying us back for the humiliation of the trip." He said thoughtfully.

Nobody could think what to do with the toothbrushes until the office messenger suggested that they would make large sturdy teaspoons. So they were distributed to nearby villagers who were advised to tie them in the centre of their huts for communal use. They are probably still hanging there today, a symbol of First World ignorance and arrogance.

The critical turn of events came in 1992 when the Catholic Bishops of Malawi issued a Pastoral Letter condemning President Banda. This touched off demonstrations throughout the country and donor countries threatened to cut off all non-humanitarian aid until Banda relinquished power.

CHAPTER THIRTY-TWO
FIRST FLAWS OF FREEDOM

Ted telephoned Sinclair at 6 am.

"Going to be big trouble today Sinclair, the Junior Civil Servants are rioting against the high-handed behaviour of the Young Pioneers. Trouble is our leader has given the Young Pioneers authority to push people around, rather like the Hitler Youth. Won't do at all. Goes right against tradition. Tradition that he forgot about when he was making bucks doctoring the people of Willesden in London. This could be nasty Sinclair so let's get to the office early and see if we can persuade the staff to stay at work and stay safe."

But when they got to the office Makwecha was already drilling his little platoon; a rather motley little army armed with a colourful assortment of weapons from chair legs to hoe handles.

"Charles Chilwa, put that set-square and metal rule back in the art-room," Sinclair shouted sternly. "You can use those bits of old furniture in the storeroom." There was no persuading them to stay, "we have to teach these children a lesson," Koma Koma said firmly and off the EAB platoon went.

Nkandawire led the volunteers out of the office and up to the Secretariat where they were meeting with other rioters prior to all marching out onto the Blantyre Road. They expected to meet the Young Pioneers en route.

'Think I'll pop home and get my ciné camera.' Sinclair thought to himself and was soon back, just in time to film the roaring mob as it poured down the hill past the Post Office. All that was missing were the spears, the skins and the shields. It was awesome.

However all too late he realised in the excitement of the occasion he had not put a film in the camera. He saw his office staff running past and called them over. "Hold on chaps, bit of a problem here, I've made a horrible mistake, the camera is not ready. Do you mind going back up to the Secretariat and running down again - and give it real stick this time!"

"OK bwana Brown," they shouted obligingly, and give it stick they did with Charles Chilwa burning the new Malawian flag with a flourish right in front of the camera. However he was wise enough to wear a scarf over his face.

When Sinclair told Ted about the re-run he smiled. "Just about says it all doesn't it?" However the riot did turn ugly and the next day many of the staff turned up battered and bruised and late for work. Koma Koma was in hospital with a badly broken arm but it did seem that the Civil Servants had won the first round.

"But watch it," said Ted. "Kamuzu will not accept defeat. The Young Pioneers will be ordered to strike back and probably have a go at any whites on the Blantyre Road today." Sinclair turned white. "My

God!" he choked, "Cynthia is driving over to Blantyre today." He rushed home but she had already left and the police refused to send out a car. The Young Pioneers were apparently stoning their cars as well.

Sinclair was frantic with worry. He could not drive over to Blantyre because Cynthia had the car. Thank God the children were still away at boarding school. He could only hope and pray that Cynthia would not be harmed.

Just when he thought he would have to ask Ted to help him search for his darling wife, the car drove in the gate. Cynthia rushed in through the front door. "Sinclair, I've had the most amazing experience." "Hold on old girl, are you alright?" Sinclair could not see any obvious injuries to wife or car. "Let's have a drink, I've been frantic with worry."

Gin and tonic in hand, they went out to the swing seat on the khondi. The evening breeze rose up from the valley and the smell of village fires blended with the delicious perfume of a Yesterday, Today and To-morrow bush by the side of the veranda.

"OK", said Sinclair, "Fire away."

Cynthia's story was an amazing one. "Well I drove off from the house thinking that I was leaving the Civil Service riot behind me, not realising that the Young Pioneers were on the war-path coming in from Blantyre. Suddenly, just by the Henderson's farm, I saw a roadblock and it was too late to turn round. So I stopped and almost immediately some very angry Young Pioneers surrounded the car. They started to rock the car, wanted to turn it over apparently. However, I remembered what you said about keeping your head and talking in a very calm way if I ever got into a sticky corner."

Sinclair gave her a squeeze. "Good girl," he said admiringly.

Cynthia went on. "They were very angry with Minister Chipembere, and kept saying to me ' You are Mr Chipembere and we are going to kill you.' So I slowly got out of the car, smiled and handed out some Smarties, you know how I never travel without them! - well after a while, when the Smarties ran out, I said, how can I be Mr Chipembere, am I a man?"

"So they went into a huddle and then the leader of the pack came back and said 'But maybe you are Mrs Chipembere' and then I countered with ' look at my skin, is it black?' Finally they came back and said 'but Mr. Chipembere has a white Mercedes like this one, and then I knew I had got them.'

"I stood up on the running board and said 'sit down my friends and I will tell you a story.' So I started, and Sinclair you should have seen my theatrical gestures when I began to speak. ' In this world there are many white Mercedes, far across the seas in a place called Germany where there are mountains and many, many people.' I went on and on and soon lulled them into a sort of glazed look. Eventually they agreed that I was a white woman and this was my car, but then one of them said, 'Perhaps Mr Chipembere thought that this was his car and is hiding in it'. So I pointed out that Mr Chipembere is wankulu, he must weigh 250lbs, where could he hide?"

"But they insisted on looking in the boot and the glove compartment and went round tapping the bodywork to hear possible noises of Chipembere's presence. They were all so serious but inside I was bursting with giggles. Anyway eventually I was allowed to travel on and quite a number of them ran beside the car, clapping and cheering, as I pulled away. Great eh?" Sinclair was silent, 'I don't suppose for one moment she knew how close to death she was'. "Well done old girl, you really handled it well but do me a favour next time there's a smell of trouble and you want to shop in Blantyre, check with me first. Promise?"

"OK darling, but please now let's have supper and go to bed. It's been a long day." Cynthia suddenly looked tired and Sinclair thought to himself 'she's worn out with the stress of today. We have to leave Malawi and leave soon.'

Cynthia was almost asleep when Sinclair finally came back into the sitting room. "Wake up old darling, time for bed, you've had a long day, fancy a cup of cocoa?" He gave her a bear hug and a kiss and whispered in her ear. "I really am very proud of you darling." But she was already asleep.

Two years later President Hastings Kamuzu Banda finally accepted the will of the people and prepared to stand down from office. At last the voice of the people was heard through the democratic ballot and Banda was effectively removed by a 2 to 1 voting ratio. Despite the brief threat of a military coup in May 1994, elections went ahead the following year. Dr Hastings Banda announced his retirement from active politics in August 1994 and died 26 November 1997.

CHAPTER THIRTY THREE
WHITE ANT FINAL REPORT

Two years later, far away from Malawi on a small farm in the Yorkshire dales, Sinclair walked up to the top of the hill above his farmhouse. He ran his hands along the dry-stone walls and took a deep breath. If he really thought about it he could almost smell the dry aromatic magic of the African bush. What do I miss most! Was it the village fires and the smell of sadza and relish, maybe the fish drying in the hot sun on the shores of Lake Malawi. 'O dear God, will I ever stop missing Africa!'

Then he felt something run across his hand; looking down he saw a column of determined ants walking from anywhere to nowhere. He watched as they changed direction for no apparent reason and then bent down to look more closely. 'Good heavens, they seem to be shaking hands'. He laughed to himself. 'Another bunch of international experts on a three day visit. Poor old ants, perhaps they have to suffer fools gladly too.'

Suddenly he was overcome with a deep sense of sadness and leaning down he picked up his old walking stick and rubbed it lovingly. Given to him as a parting present by his friend Chief Jakob, it remained one of his most prized possessions. 'Ah well', he thought, 'Life may never be the same but maybe a different life, with different possibilities!'

He put his hand down into the path of the ants. The column stopped, had a conference and then some ants walked round his fingers, while others went under his hand. A few brave ones climbed over his knuckles pausing in a brave gesture of leg waving. Sinclair laughed. 'Well, well, black, red or white, ants seem to have a common characteristic, determination. Thanks for the lesson little buddies. I must get to know the Yorkshire ants now but will you ever be able to help me forget the white ants of Africa? I don't think so.'

Sinclair Brown set off back down the hill to Cynthia, the children, his waiting supper and his new way of life. He knew that his memories of Malawi would never dim. No matter how well he adapted to change he would always know that part of him was in Africa forever. New or different, it could be a challenge, but it will never be the same. He straightened his shoulders and walked quickly into the warmth and safety of his family.

HISTORICAL NOTES

THE GREAT DIVIDE

In 1884, three European countries, England, France and Germany held a low-key conference, called The Congress of Berlin. It was held to discuss and agree on how to split up Africa between them. Not surprisingly no African representatives were invited!

France ended up with the most land with England in second place. However, as far as the English were concerned, the French could keep the land they fancied. In their opinion, the French had ended up with 'a huge desert with insignificant minerals, occupied by Muslim fundamentalists'.

Whereas the English, largely thanks to the ruthless Cecil John Rhodes, with the support of Queen Victoria, eventually captured a number of magnificent countries ranging from the Sudan and Somaliland in the North; Gambia, Sierra Leone, Gold Coast and Nigeria in the West; Kenya, Uganda, Tanganyika and Zanzibar in the East; South West Africa (Namibia) and Bechuanaland in the South West; Central Africa; later to be divided up into Northern and Southern Rhodesia and Nyasaland; with the biggest prize of all being the Union of South Africa in the South, where Rhodes and his friends found and secured some of the world's largest deposits of gold and diamonds.

POTTED HISTORY OF AN AREA OF CENTRAL AFRICA DESIGNATED AS 'UNKNOWN TERRITORY' ON ANCIENT MAPS

Hominids are known to have inhabited the area, which became known as Maravi, for some two million years. In fact the remains of human settlements dating back some 100 000 years have been discovered recently on the shores of the massive lake which covers almost a fifth of Malawi's land mass and lies in the trough of the Great Rift Valley which runs north to south down the length of the country.

Called Lake Nyasa (Lake Lake) in error by early settlers (nyasa was the local word for lake), today it is called Lake Malawi and is the third largest natural lake in Africa. The ancient name of the country, Maravi, loosely translated "shining or reflected water" is thought to have referred to the visual effect of the evening sun sparkling on the lake.

Evidence suggests that those roving Stone Age residents were the same Boskopoid people who occupied much of this part of Africa at that time, the ancestors of the pygmies of Central Africa and the San (Bushmen) of Southern Africa, who now survive only in isolated pockets.

The early 19th century brought two significant migrations with the Yao from Portuguese East Africa, armed by the Arab slave traders, capturing Maravian inhabitants and selling them into slavery. About the same time groups of Zulu warriors from southern Africa began to invade Maravi and eventually spread through the whole area, overpowering many local tribes.

The first Europeans to arrive in the country were the Portuguese explorers who reached the African interior from the east coast of Portuguese East Africa. The most famous British explorer to reach this area was David Livingstone, a Scottish missionary who first travelled to the country in 1859.

Soon signs of international commercial colonialisation were seen with the formation of the Livingstone Central African Mission Company in 1878 that was briefed to develop a river route into Central Africa and introduce general trade to the region.

The British Government declared the Shire Highlands a Protectorate in 1889 and expanded its holdings to include much of the land on the western side of what is Lake Malawi today. In 1907 the new colony was named NYASALAND and on 11 May 1914, the formal grant of a Nyasaland Coat of Arms was declared. Over the next forty years a growing number of African leaders rose up against the colonial rule and were crushed and in some cases executed. In January 1915, the Rev. John Chilembwe headed an uprising that eventually collapsed after his church was destroyed. He was shot by a border patrol as he attempted to escape through the Fort Lister gap to Portuguese territory. However it was not until 1953 that the Nyasaland African Congress was established and Dr. Hastings Banda requested to accept an out-of-country leadership. This decision came about as the result of a deeply resented British decision to include Nyasaland within the Federation of Northern and Southern Rhodesia.

DOCTOR HASTINGS BANDA

Born and raised in the Central Region of Nyasaland, Hastings Banda went to work in neighbouring Rhodesia in 1915 and then onto the gold mines of South Africa. By 1925 having saved enough money to travel to the USA, he took up a scholarship at the Wilberforce Institute, Ohio and from there went to the University of Chicago and on to a medical college in Nashville, Tennessee, where he qualified as a medical doctor in 1937. In order to fulfil his ambition to practice medicine in Great Britain, he acquired further qualifications in Edinburgh, Scotland, and set up a practice in the north of England eventually moving it to Willesden in London.

NGWAZI HASTINGS KAMUZU BANDA
Life President of Malawi from 1964 to 1994

In 1953 he established a practice in the Gold Coast (now Ghana).

In 1955, the NAC (Nyasaland African Congress), under the radical leadership of Henry Chipembere and Kanyama Chiume, invited Banda home to lead the country to independence. However, it was not until 1958 that he returned to Nyasaland.

It was said that the reason why he always addressed political meetings and rallies through an interpreter was that he could not speak Chinyanja well. Perhaps during the forty-three years he was out of the country the language had developed and changed to the extent that he felt a lack of fluency would inhibit his powers of rhetoric. Certainly Banda's dynamic personality and almost godlike leadership qualities fired up a national campaign that culminated in civil disorder and riots in March 1959. The authorities declared a state of emergency, banning the NAC and arresting its leaders. Dr Banda was detained and escorted to Rhodesia where he remained in prison for nearly a year.

However, in 1960 the British Government capitulated and Dr Hastings Banda was deported to the land of his birth where he was welcomed at Chilaka Airport by thousands of cheering supporters. Later that year a constitutional conference was held with elections taking place in August. The Malawi Congress party won overwhelmingly. Full self-government was attained in January 1963 and Doctor Hastings Kamuzu Banda was declared the Prime Minister of Malawi.

On 31 December 1963 the hated Federation of Northern and Southern Rhodesia and Nyasaland was dissolved and the independent state of Malawi was declared on 6 July 1964. The country became a republic and one-party state on 6 July 1966 and Doctor Hastings Kamuzu Banda was 'crowned' President of Malawi at a glittering ceremony held in a massive stadium packed with international representatives.

Doctor Banda's original term of office as President of Malawi was extended to a Life-President tenancy in 1971.

It soon became obvious that President Banda did not intend sharing the power of rule and final decision with his ministers. This led to a revolt by a group of top ministers resulting in some of them fleeing the country. The group of rebels included Henry Chipembere who went to America, Kanyama Chiume to Zambia and Yatuta Chizisa to Tanzania.

Down through the 1980s President Banda tightened the reins of control over the country giving him enormous power over the people and the development of the country. He assumed a god-like role, linking himself and his plans for Malawi with the concept of the country itself. Furthermore he took over the running of all the major ministries together with the political machine; the ruling party and the economy. Any government ministers and officials who questioned his authority were ruthlessly imprisoned or killed

It was estimated that by the 1990s some 250,000 people had disappeared or had been murdered during Banda's thirty-one-year-reign. However by this time opposition to his totalitarian one-party rule had grown, spurred on by the end of the Cold War and the withdrawal of international aid to the Third World.

The critical turn in events came when in 1992 the Catholic Bishops of Malawi issued a Pastoral Letter condemning Banda. This touched off a series of demonstrations throughout the country and donor countries threatened to cut off all non-humanitarian aid unless Banda agree to relinquish power.

President Banda finally accepted the will of the people and prepared to stand down from office. Despite the brief threat of a military coup elections went ahead in May 1994 and at last the voice of the population was heard through the democratic

ballot.

President Banda announced his retirement from active politics in August 1994. He died on 26 November 1997 leaving a vast fortune reportedly to his official hostess and companion, Cecilia Tamanda Kadzamira. However since his Will has never been found, the distribution of the eventual benefits is still locked within legal discussion and conflict.

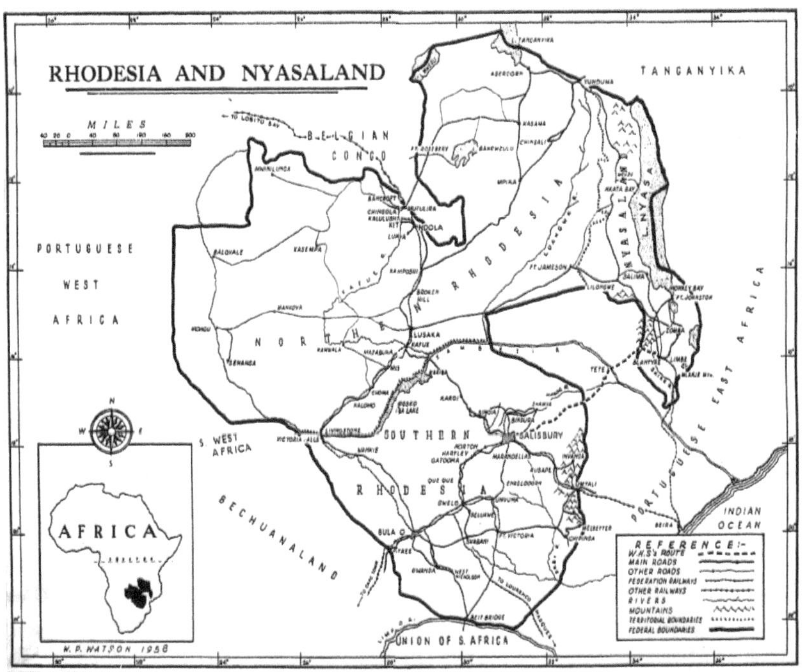

MAP OF THE PROTECTORATE OF RHODESIA AND NYASALAND

Temperature

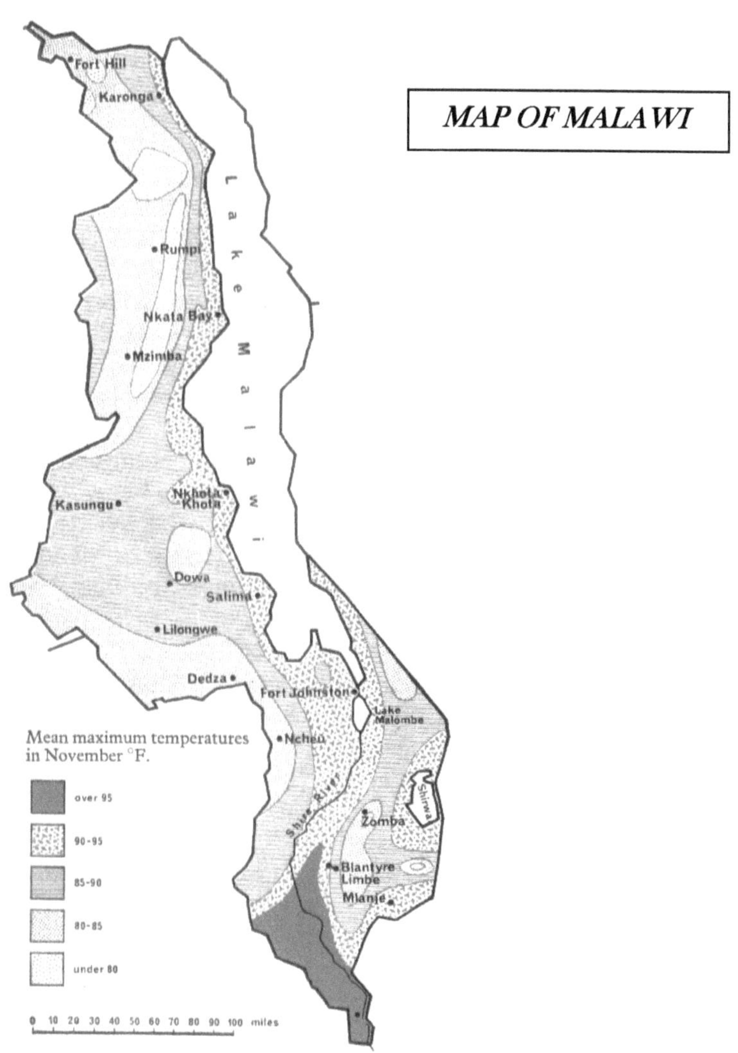

MAP OF MALAWI

DATA ON MALAWI

The landmass of Malawi is approximately 36,100 square miles. It is a strip of land some 520 miles long, varying in widths from 50 to 100 miles wide and roughly conforming to the shape of Lake Malawi that covers more than a fifth of the country.

Malawi is an independent republic with a democratic government. It forms part of the Southern African Region and is landlocked between Mozambique, Zambia and Tanzania. Malawi is reported to be one of the World's least developed countries. The capital city is Lilongwe with Blantyre and Zomba ranking as two of the oldest towns in the country. There is a population of 10,701,824 (July 2002,) spread across the three regions, Northern, Central and Southern.

The official languages are Chichewa and English and the local currency is the Malawian Kwacha. The economy is predominately agricultural, with about 90% of the population living in the rural areas. Agriculture accounts for 40% of GDP and 88% of export revenues. Exports include tea, coffee, tobacco, cotton and groundnuts.

There is one rainy season with the dry season extending from May to October but there is a wide diversity of seasonal weather over the four climatic zones.

ACKNOWLEDGEMENT - SOURCE OF DATA

HISTORICAL FACTS
National Archives UK/Zimbabwe:
www.nationalarchives.gov.uk
www.empiremuseum.co.uk

MAP OF RHODESIA AND NYASALAND:
W.P. Watson 1958 - extract MY LIFE by W. Stansfield.

MAP OF MALAWI AND DATA:
www.irisministeries.co.uk

PHOTOGRAPHS: the late Derrick Arnall / Patricia Bean

DISCLAIMER

I, Patricia Shelagh Pink, formerly Patricia Shelagh Bean, formerly Patricia Shelagh McDermott lived in Nyasaland/Malawi from 1961 to 1969. During those years I worked for a Government Department and became actively involved in the sporting and social life of Zomba.

I wrote a yearly diary of events whilst living in Zomba and, over the years, have kept in touch with many of my Zomba work associates and personal friends; therefore I am fully aware that it is possible that my story of events and characters may open up flashes of memory in the minds of my colleagues and become a matter of concern.

I must emphasise that The Last of the White Ants has been written as an acknowledgement of those extraordinary years that led to the birth of Malawi. It is also a belated and much deserved accolade to the dedicated service given to Nyasaland/Malawi by the British Overseas Civil Service personnel. My years in Zomba left me with a lasting admiration for the British White Ants and I wanted to ensure that they would always be remembered.

Perhaps the main difference between this book and other books, which have been written on the country, is that this one is written around employees bound by the Civil Service rules where work and social behaviour were concerned. Employees yes, but also human beings who managed, despite the limitations of their surroundings, to spice their private lives with competitiveness, a great variety of activities and creativities, much laughter and a few tears. Who could blame them for occasionally stepping off the straight and narrow?

I apologise for any inaccuracies and unfair judgement of people and events. Any possible similarity between past residents of Zomba, living or dead, and the characters portrayed in my book, THE LAST OF THE WHITE ANTS, is purely coincidental.

www.ingramcontent.com/pod-product-compliance
Lightning Source LLC
Chambersburg PA
CBHW030343310726
48979CB00001B/160

9781425191665